The Village of Lost Souls

The Village of Lost Souls

Sam Kates

SMITHCRAFT
PRESS

All characters appearing in this work are fictitious.
Any resemblance to real persons, living or dead,
is purely coincidental.

Printed in the United States of America. First edition, December 2012.
Smithcraft Press edition, March 2014.

ISBN 978-1-62927-009-8

Smithcraft Press
1921 Michels Drive NE
Palm Bay, FL 32905

www.SmithcraftPress.com

Contents

Desolation

The village haunts me. It seeps into my consciousness and invades my dreams.

I went back there. I wanted to banish the ghosts.

The village no longer exists.

I forced my way through brambles and ferns, past springy saplings, moving carefully to avoid spraining an ankle on hidden rubble. Dandelion heads blew like swirling snowflakes across my vision.

Nature was reclaiming its own.

But still the birds did not sing.

I stood where my aunt's house had once proudly reared towards the sky. Impulsively, I stooped and tore away undergrowth at my feet. I arose, holding a fragment of jet slate that gave the house its name. I stared at it for a moment, turning it over in my fingers, before letting it fall to be concealed for all time.

The pond had disappeared too, choked by silt and weed.

I thought of her then. For an instant, she was before me, hair as black as the fragment of slate, eyes round and smouldering, red lips turned up into that sensuous smile

"I love you, John," she said.

Brushing wetness from my grizzled cheeks, I turned and walked away.

I had returned in search of peace. I found only a reflection of my heart's desolation.

The Fight

It is difficult to be certain when the events and the telling are separated by such a span of time, but I suppose that it all started with a fight.

I was the youngest of three children. My brother, Callum, was nine when I made my entrance into this world in 1930. My sister, Morfydd, was five.

Dark and sturdy, my sister inherited Ma's fiery Welsh temper when roused. Legs planted firmly apart, one hand on hip, she would wag her forefinger at the object of her ire as her tongue delivered pointed slivers of reproach that could make the recipient cringe. I saw boys twice her size wilt under the force of her rage. Fortunately for the male youth of Newcastle-upon-Tyne, it took a great deal for my sister to unleash her temper and she mellowed as she grew older. She would have developed into a fine woman, good-natured, loving and loyal. She never had the chance. The war claimed her before she reached her twenties.

Callum took after our father, a gentle man who was never quick to temper unless very sorely provoked. Da's distaste for violence and strong language was all the more surprising when considering his upbringing in a working-class district of Glasgow and his employment in Tyneside as a docker.

Callum was my hero. Tall for his age, he towered over me like a demi-god. Possessing Da's unassuming manner and quiet charm, not to mention his rugged good looks, Callum was popular with his peers, male and female alike. He and Morfydd were very close; he would do anything to protect her. As I grew old enough to appreciate such things, I knew that he would do the same for me.

Most of my childhood memories are hazy or fractured, really nothing more than snippets. Except for one. I can recall with a clarity that hasn't dimmed over the many intervening years the time that Callum fought the Mahoney brothers.

I was about five when the fight took place, which would put Callum at around fourteen. He had taken me and Morfydd to the scruffy piece of wasteground, two streets from our house, which the local kids would pretend was St James's Park, home of Newcastle United Football Club. It was a late summer evening and dusk was approaching as the two teams hammered away at each other's goal, two rolled-up jumpers placed on the ground a few yards apart. That evening Callum played for the 'away' team, Sunderland, and the Mahoney brothers were all in the Newcastle team.

They were a fearsome bunch, those Mahoneys. The eldest was Mitch, so called because he was never in school. The Mitcher Man (or Truancy Officer to give him his correct title) had given up trying to make Mitch attend school years ago. Mitch was nearly fifteen and more than a match for most boys his age—and, indeed, many older than him—in a fist fight. He was built like a brick shithouse, as we used to say: not particularly tall but almost as wide, with a barrel-shaped torso constructed of solid muscle, supported by legs as wide around the thigh as my five-year-old waist. Mitch later had a spell with a travelling fair as a bare-knuckle fighter, with a great deal of success so we heard, before the war arrived and interrupted everyone's careers.

Mitch's brothers were younger than him by three and five years, although they were showing signs of filling out to the same dense shape as Mitch.

That summer evening, I was tired and irritable, a fairly normal state for a five-year-old as bedtime approached. I sat on the ground alongside Morfydd and watched the football for a time without complaint. Then I began to long for home and the comfort of Ma's lap. I started to whine and tug at Morfydd, getting to my feet and nagging her to call Callum to take us home. She could see that the game was tense with Newcastle, losing 8-9, pressing for the equaliser before darkness stopped play. She tried to shush me with a hug, but she was no substitute for my mother. I started crying and called out to Callum.

At that moment, Mitch happened to be running past the spot where I stood at the edge of the playing area. Zealously competitive as he was, Mitch must have been afraid that Callum would leave and thus bring the match to a premature end before his team could tie the score. I tell you, football is serious business in Newcastle.

Mitch skidded to a halt. He raised one great ham fist and whacked me around the ear. I doubt that he even considered what he was doing but acted upon instinct, much as he did with his own brothers.

There were gasps from the other players. Mitch had overstepped the mark. Even in those rough times, it was not on for a boy to strike a playmate's younger brother. That was the older brother's sole prerogative. Not that Callum had ever felt compelled to exercise it.

Mitch's blow cut off my whimpering in mid flow. Luckily for me, Mitch had not put anything like his full power into the clout. My ear throbbed and felt uncommonly hot, but it was the shock of being struck by one of my brother's friends that stunned me into keeping my mouth firmly shut. I understood enough to realise that Callum could not ignore the violation.

Morfydd scrambled to her feet, looking scared and uncertain. I scrabbled at her dress until she grasped my hand and held it tight. Never one short of words, she too was stung into silence.

Mitch stared at me. His eyes grew wide as realisation stole across his broad features. Even had he been the apologising sort, he knew, as every child present knew, that Callum could not accept an apology and forget about it. The issue could only be settled in that time-honoured playground tradition: the fistfight. I believe that Mitch genuinely regretted striking me. Not because of the inevitable consequences—he had never been one to shy away from the rough stuff, and often instigated it—but that he felt ashamed of the act itself. Still, it was done and could not be undone.

Mitch shrugged his shoulders.

"Oops," he muttered.

He turned to face my brother.

Callum strode towards us. The other boys, the match forgotten, wordlessly gathered behind him and followed. As Callum halted in front of Mitch, the others formed a loose semi-circle and waited. The expressions on their faces were anticipatory, lustful, like hyenas about to gorge on carrion. There is an unwritten code of honour in the playground and these boys knew it had been breached. It could only be remedied with the use of fists. It mattered little who won the fight, only that there be a fight. That was the way things were.

My brother slowly raised his fists into the classical boxer's stance. He said nothing, but his steely grey eyes bored into Mitch. It is one of my abiding memories of Callum, standing there on that patch of wasteground in the fading light, the breeze ruffling his deep-brown hair, his expression one of grim resolution as he beckoned his opponent on with his eyes. He looked so noble and downright heroic, and I loved him at that moment with a strength and clarity that has barely faded over the years. At the same time, I was scared for him.

Although some months younger than Mitch, Callum was a good six inches taller with a far superior reach. His willowy frame belied a wiry strength and feline agility. Da had taught him boxing and wrestling together with some less ethical moves for use in times of dire need. This was more than likely one of those times.

I had seen Mitch Mahoney fight once before. It had not been a pretty sight. Callum had let me watch for a few minutes before whisking me away home, but it had been long enough. Mitch fought like a wounded tiger. He employed any means at his disposal to maim his opponent. He punched, squeezed, scrammed, kicked, bit, gouged and pummelled. He used any part of his anatomy that happened to be handy—forehead, elbows, knees, heels, teeth, thumbs—to inflict pain. He was one of the most feared boys in the area, even among older youths, and for good reason. I was afraid he would kill Callum.

Mitch's brothers formed part of the semi-circle of bodies behind Callum. As my brother squared up to Mitch, one of them broke the silence by shouting a message of encouragement to Mitch.

It was enough to spur him into action. He lowered his head and charged at Callum with frightening speed. For a split second, it looked as though that initial headlong rush would end it there and then. Mitch would catch Callum in the midriff and his bulk would bowl my brother to the ground where Mitch could immediately bring to bear his repertoire of dirty tricks. As Morfydd yanked me out of harm's way, my bladder nearly let go, so certain was I that the game was already up for Callum.

Mitch was fast, astoundingly so for one so bulky. Callum was even faster. At the last possible instant before Mitch enveloped him, Callum deftly stepped aside. Mitch clutched at air, his momentum carrying him on. As Mitch shot past him, Callum aimed a short, straight right that connected with a dull slap to Mitch's left ear. There was a sharp intake of breath from the onlookers and I felt the excitement go up a notch.

It should have ended there. Callum had repaid with interest the blow that Mitch had dealt to me and it should have been enough to satisfy the playground code of honour. I thought they would shake hands and call it quits. That was until I saw Mitch's expression.

Mitch stopped in his tracks and turned slowly to face Callum. His ear must have been smarting from the force of Callum's blow but he made no move to rub it. His eyes were alive with excitement and a grin approaching rapture creased his face. His bloodlust fully aroused, Mitch looked vibrant, as if the very purpose of his existence was being fulfilled. Callum must have known in that moment that there was no chance of ending it quickly. The reason for their fight had become irrelevant. It was enough for Mitch that there was a fight. Everyone present could see that Mitch would scrap until he or Callum dropped.

Callum did not waste breath speaking. He simply stood and waited.

He didn't have to wait long. Mitch charged him again, less wildly this time and ready for my brother's side-step. As Mitch approached, Callum tensed as though to spring aside once more. Mitch's eyes darted to the side in anticipation but Callum stood his ground and pole-axed Mitch with a right hook that sent a shudder through the onlookers. Mitch thudded to the soft ground with a splat, left cheekbone already swelling.

I couldn't help myself. I squealed and jumped up and down on the spot, nearly wetting myself once more. I felt Morfydd's hands on my shoulders and her breath on my ear.

"Hush, Johnny!" she hissed. "It's not over yet. Look at Mitch!"

Mitch was sitting on the ground, shaking his bear-like head. His grin widened. His left eye was rapidly closing, giving his beatific expression a lopsided, manic look. He lumbered to his feet. This time he walked towards Callum, his arms raised to protect his face as he approached within range of my brother's fists.

The battle proper began.

It must have continued for at least ten minutes, although it seemed much shorter to us looking on. Callum made his greater height and agility count. He inflicted more damage to Mitch Mahoney in that one fight than had been inflicted upon him in countless previous fights combined. But it was not one-way traffic. Mitch achieved some measure of success on the few occasions that he was able to penetrate Callum's guard. One of Callum's eyes was also closed, his lips and cheek wet with blood, and he grimaced as he moved as though one of his ribs was cracked. But Callum could be thankful that the fight was taking place in open space where he had room to keep skipping out of reach and avoid too much close-quarter stuff. Mitch's sheer bulk, brute strength and enthusiasm for confrontation would have quickly overwhelmed Callum in a confined space.

Night-time had almost completely fallen. The sky was clear and the stars that twinkled into view provided sufficient light to illuminate the combatants as they continued to batter away at each other. I watched transfixed, clinging tight to Morfydd's hand. We both knew better than to run to fetch an adult to stop the fight. Much as neither of us wanted our brother to be hurt, Callum would resent our interference. We feared that resentment more than his pain. Besides, young and inexperienced as we were in the art of pugilism, we could tell that Callum was inflicting far more damage than he was sustaining and the end of the fight was nigh. This must have also been apparent to the other onlookers.

Morfydd noticed first. I heard her sharp intake of breath and sensed her stiffen. I followed her gaze. Through the gloom, I could make out two figures that had detached themselves from the cluster of boys that followed every blow of the fight with rapt attention. The two figures tentatively approached Callum and Mitch, who were too engrossed with each other to notice them. As the two interlopers circled behind Callum, I realised who they were: the younger Mahoney brothers. As their identities became clear, so did their intentions. They each meant to grab one of Callum's arms from behind, giving their older brother free access to Callum's face and body. Although I have sometimes wondered about it, at that moment there was no doubt in my mind that Mitch would take full advantage of such an opening.

I drew a deep breath and yelled at the top of my shrill voice, "Callum! Look out behind you!"

Callum whirled around just as the younger Mahoneys were reaching out to grab his arms. He reacted to the new threat upon instinct. He drove a fist into each of their faces, rocking them backwards. But his attention had swayed from Mitch who seized his chance. Mitch leapt onto Callum's back, the full force of his considerable weight bearing Callum face-first to the ground, tearing the breath from his lungs. Mitch sat astride Callum, gripping his ribs between his knees like he would a horse, and began to rain club-like blows onto Callum's head, neck and shoulders. The two younger

Mahoneys rallied and aimed kicks at any exposed part of my brother they could reach.

Low mutterings came from the crowd of boys but not one of them made any move to help Callum. It was left to Morfydd and me to provide what little aid we could.

Screaming, "Cowards!", Morfydd dragged me forwards and ran at Mitch Mahoney. Releasing my hand, she attempted to shove Mahoney off Callum's back. She might as well have tried to move a mountain. Mitch raised one hand and contemptuously flapped her away as if he were swatting a fly. Morfydd thudded to the ground on her bottom with a surprised yelp.

I attempted to grab hold of one of the younger Mahoney's legs. It was like trying to grab a swaying tree trunk. I too was simply brushed aside. I lay where I fell, sobbing with frustration at my inability to do anything to prevent my brother's annihilation. Callum did not stand a chance pinned to the ground with Mitch pounding the back of his head and the other two laying in with their feet. But Callum had other ideas.

Seeing the way that both Morfydd and I had been summarily dealt with injected into Callum a fresh surge of rage and energy. Ignoring the kicks of the younger Mahoneys, Callum braced his arms on the ground and heaved upwards with all his might. So confident was Mitch that Callum was beaten, the manoeuvre caught him completely by surprise. Mitch first lurched ungainly to one side, then was thrown clear as Callum surged upright.

Morfydd was just rising to her feet as Mitch's bulk thudded to the ground next to her. She didn't hesitate. Leaping high into the air, she tucked her feet beneath her as she fell. She landed squarely upon Mitch's stomach with her knees, driving the air from his lungs in a startled "Whoof!"

Terrified at what Mitch would do to her, I scrambled to my feet and pulled her away before he could recover. My urgency was unnecessary. Mitch writhed and squirmed on the ground, eyes rolling, gasping desperately for breath. He looked for all the world like a stranded fish.

Callum's expression as he turned to face the younger Mahoneys was one of such seething anger that they took an involuntary step back. Callum swarmed at them, fists pistoning with short, powerful jabs. They had only to separate to prevent Callum from taking them out together, but they were so disorientated by the speed and ferocity of Callum's onslaught that they backed away side by side, trying to cover up in vain. Within seconds they were bloodied and bowed, the fight beaten from them.

Callum hissed between his teeth, "Get out of here! Both of you! *Now*!"

They needed no second invitation. Turning tail, they fled, leaving their older brother to face Callum's wrath alone.

Callum watched them disappear into the twilight through narrowed eyes. Then he turned and strode towards Mitch, his shoulders set and his fists clenched. Mitch had managed to clamber to his knees, but was doubled over, breath coming in ragged gasps. Callum stood and waited, ignoring the odd shout from the onlookers to finish Mitch off. At last Mitch gained some control over his breathing and rose shakily to his feet. He eyed my brother and, for the first time since Mitch had struck me to set the whole thing in motion, they spoke to each other.

"Well then, Callum," said Mitch.

"Well then, Mitch." Callum sounded calm, but I could tell from the tension in his stance that fire still raged in his belly.

"You fight well." There was a note of grudging admiration in Mitch's voice. My heart sank at his next words. "But I'm not finished yet. Ready to go some more?"

"Aye."

I turned away as they squared up to one another again. I could not stand to see Callum suffer more harm and I hid my face in my hands. Clearly, Morfydd was of the same mind.

"No!" she shouted. "No more!" She strode forward belligerently, a slight girl, barely ten years old. The starlight picked out her pale features beneath her mop of curly black hair as she stood between Callum and Mitch, a dwarf between two giants, and glowered at them.

"I'm telling you Callum Andrews, and you Mitch Mahoney, that's enough!" She nodded in my direction before glaring at Callum. "You've more than paid Mitch back for slapping John." She glanced sternly at Mitch. "You've more than defended your honour, or whatever you call it." She raised one arm and pointed a finger at each of them in turn. "If you carry on fighting now, it's only because you're both too pig-headed to know when enough's enough. Everyone here knows it too." She glared pointedly at the boys who stood watching. "But nobody else has the balls to come out and say it."

The onlooking boys shuffled their feet and stole quick glances at each other. One of them cleared his throat and spoke.

"She's right, Mitch, Callum. You've a'ready hit lumps out of each other. Unless you stop, one of you will end up seriously hurt. We don't want to see that happen, and Cal's kid brother certainly shouldn't. Take him home, man." A murmur of agreement arose from the other boys.

Morfydd shot a look of gratitude to the speaker. She regarded Callum and Mitch, hands planted on her hips. "Well, what about it?" she demanded.

The tension drained from Callum's stance. He shrugged his shoulders and looked Mitch in the eye.

"I'm willing to end it here if you are," he said.

Mitch took a moment to consider his reply.

"Let's just call it the end of round one, shall we?"

He stepped forward and held out his right hand. Callum gripped it. He stared grimly at Mitch.

"Say the word and we'll start round two. You know where to find me."

"Aye, that I do."

Mitch grinned but the smile never reached his one open eye. He turned on his heel and strode away into the darkness without glancing back. Callum watched Mitch go, his lips pressed into a thin line. He knew that he and Mitch weren't finished yet.

He was right too, although their next encounter would also be their final one. It took place when I was seventeen.

By then, Callum had been dead for over seven years.

War

The storm clouds of war had been gathering over Europe for months. On September 3rd 1939, they broke. I remember the tingling sensation that coursed through my 9-year-old body as Chamberlain's words played over the airways. Judging by the grim expressions on the faces of my parents and siblings as we huddled around the wireless, my family did not share my anticipation. They knew what the announcement was likely to mean in terms of loss of life and hardship, although I doubt that any of them thought the war would last anywhere near six years or exact such a hefty toll.

To me, the war meant just one thing: excitement.

At the height of the war, I asked my mother if she believed Hitler to be a man of pure evil. Her answer surprised me.

"No," she said. "I don't believe there's any such thing as pure evil in this world. Nor pure goodness." Ma was in the process of darning a thick woolly sock. She made a little extra cash—'pin money' she called it—to supplement Da's wages from the docks by taking in sewing from merchant crewmen who had better ways to spend their time ashore than mending their own clothes. Now she placed the sock and needle to one side and regarded me soberly.

"Listen closely to me, John. Every single one of us has the capacity to do both good and evil. And every single one of us, from the most wicked monster to the most pious priest, will at some point in his life carry out a kind deed or commit a sin. There is no absolute black or white. There are just varying shades of grey."

"But, Ma," I protested, "Hitler's the most evil man that's ever lived."

Ma shrugged. "Maybe he is. That's not our judgement to make. I am sure that he represents a very dark shade of grey... but black? Even he contains the capacity for goodness. He may choose not to use it, but that's what makes us human—our ability to *choose* our path through life."

"But people are saying he's killed millions of Jews," I went on. "That must make Hitler worse than the Devil. And besides," I added, "Charlie Watts says that Hitler's mother was a jackal and his rise to power was foretold in the Bible."

"Charlie Watts is *twp*," retorted Ma, her Welsh roots becoming evident in the heat of debate. "Even if those terrible rumours about the Jews are true, God forbid, I still wouldn't regard Hitler as the Devil incarnate. An even darker shade of grey, yes. If a person truly possessed a black soul, it would leave no room for him to be redeemed. I have faith that everyone, no matter how evil, can beg forgiveness when he comes face to face with his Creator. And He will forgive. We all have some goodness within us. It may be well hidden in some but it's there nonetheless. After all, He has to have something to work with. And there lies our salvation."

Ma leaned forward and took my hands in hers. Her eyes glistened as they looked deeply into mine.

"We have to have hope, John," she said. "There has to be a spark of goodness, however tiny, in everyone to make it worth the struggle. And it is a struggle . . . I sometimes wonder how much more pain we can endure." A single tear breached her eyelid and rolled gently down her cheek. She ignored it.

"Whilst there is goodness, there is hope," she said. "Without hope, we have nothing, *cariad*, nothing. Except despair."

Neville Chamberlain had barely finished announcing to the nation that war had been declared on Nazi Germany when Callum made an announcement of his own. He intended to join the army.

I was not in the least bit surprised. I expected nothing less of my brother who had become a strapping eighteen-year-old, over six feet tall, broad of shoulder and narrow of waist. Since his fight with the Mahoney brothers, my hero-worship of Callum had grown to epic proportions. I saw him as my all-conquering protector who would stand up to any enemy, no matter how fierce. It was perfectly natural that Callum should go off to fight the Nazis. I would have been disappointed if he had not declared his intention to enlist.

Ma and Morfydd viewed things differently. They advised Callum not to be too hasty. They reasoned that the war was unlikely to last long and he could always join up later if the initial estimate was wrong. They argued that fit young men would still be required at home and that he'd be able to make just as important a contribution to the war effort without taking up a gun. Finally, they entreated him with tears not to leave them.

Callum remained unmoved. In the calm manner that so characterised him, he informed his mother and sister that he considered it his duty as an Englishman, not to mention a Scotsman and a Welshman to boot, to join the hundreds of thousands of other young British men rushing to protect their homeland. He explained that he would not be able to look at himself in the mirror if he stayed at home while others his age were away fighting for the freedom from oppression that was their birthright. No amount of arguing, cajoling or outright emotional blackmail could shake his resolve.

Da was silent throughout the discussions. He had fought in the Great War and understood only too well the sense of duty to which Callum alluded. Had his health not been starting to fail, I am sure Da would have been tempted to enlist with Callum.

So Callum joined the army. Despite their misgivings, Ma and Morfydd could not help but admire his quiet courage, and my father visibly swelled with pride. Da never voiced it though; that was not his way. I more than made up for Da's reticence, wittering on to anyone who cared to listen, and to many who didn't, about my big brother becoming a soldier and departing for the continent to kick Hitler's head in.

Fighting involving British troops had already begun on mainland Europe when Callum received his call-up papers. They dropped through the letter box in an official brown envelope bearing the Ministry of Defence's frank. Morfydd brought the envelope through to the living room where Ma and I were finishing our breakfast at the dining table. She carried the envelope gingerly, as though it might break in her hands, or explode.

Ma glanced up and her eyes narrowed.

"Is it . . . ?"

Morfydd nodded.

Ma's lips compressed into a thin line.

"What's up?" I enquired, having no idea why the atmosphere was suddenly so tense.

"Hisht, boy!" said Ma, rising stiffly to her feet.

She took the envelope from Morfydd, examined it briefly and placed it on the mantelpiece.

"There," she said. "I'll hear no more about it."

When I came home from school that afternoon, the envelope was still there. There it remained until Callum and Da returned from the docks, tired, dirty and smelling of diesel. As they came into the living room, Ma rose and walked to the mantelpiece. She handed the brown envelope to Callum without a word.

Callum hesitated for only a moment, turning the envelope over once in his hands. Then he tore it open and extracted the sheet of flimsy white paper from within. When he glanced back up, his face was expressionless.

"I'm to report to Aldershot for basic training . . . er, let's see, a week tomorrow."

I couldn't understand why Ma and Morfydd burst into tears.

It was an exciting time to be nine years old. My friends and I could identify every known British and German aircraft, and this was before we had set eyes on one of the latter. War games had replaced football, temporarily at least, as our favourite pastime. Unlike football where everyone would readily agree to take it in turns to play for Sunderland, nobody was willing to act out the part of the Germans and so battles were fought against imaginary opponents. Hardly surprising that we always won.

To us, war was a great adventure where good was pitted against evil and it never entered our heads that we could lose. Even during the early days of the war, when losing was a very real possibility and civilians in the south were arming themselves against a German invasion, neither I nor my friends ever seriously contemplated us losing. How could we lose? We represented the power of goodness, they were evil, and good always triumphs over evil. End of discussion. Life is simple when you're nine.

As for the shocking numbers of dead, the brutalities, the maiming, the massacres, the devastating losses of limbs, lives and innocence, it was all above our heads. Willing ignorance was God's way of protecting children against the stark realities of bloody conflict. My friends and I existed happily in our own little world where we would aim an imaginary gun at an imaginary enemy, shout "Bang!" and he would obligingly fall down dead. Enemy bullets would only ever nick us—"I'm hit! But it's only a flesh wound. Take that . . . Bang!"—and we would live to fight another day, heroes to a boy.

It was due to that childishly simplistic and optimistic view of war, and life in general, that I remained blissfully unaware of the undercurrent of sadness that pervaded the atmosphere in our house on the evening before Callum left home for the army. Ma told me about it years later. She said that the feeling of underlying sorrow was so thick you could practically taste it, a coppery, bitter taste that overwhelmed all else and frustrated every effort to drown it beneath food or alcohol or gaiety. That did not prevent the efforts being made.

Ma made up her mind to give Callum a proper send-off. Keeping me and Morfydd home from school, she set us to work. For a week we peeled, sliced, rolled, beat, boiled, baked and drooled until our fingers were raw. Friends and neighbours all contributed ingredients with the selfless generosity that is sadly disappearing from the world. By the time that Callum's last night arrived, we had made a spread fit for royalty.

Guests started to arrive in the early evening, each caller armed with a crate of stout or pale ale, or a bottle of gin or whisky. The party was soon in full swing. And what a party!

To mask their sorrow the women drank, danced and indulged in high spirits as if they were the happiest women alive and had to prove it. The men understood and supported their womenfolk as if they too were banshees let loose for their annual night of haunting. Our house reverberated with the beat of the big bands, the thump of stomping boots, the clink of bottles and peals of raucous laughter.

I ghosted through the pandemonium, turning my head this way and that, agog at the merriment. From my viewpoint the evening was magical, a perfect send-off for my brother who seemed to revel in the atmosphere of abandonment. He danced wildly with Ma and Morfydd, spinning them around and clasping them alternately to his chest as he cavorted. Da joined in and the four of them twirled, clapped and stamped, eyes gleaming, high colour in their cheeks. Callum spotted me and, barely breaking stride, swept me up into his arms. So I became the fifth, but only unwilling, member of the Andrews Family Mad Dance Troupe but I was soon laughing along with them, clinging to my brother as we spun and whooped with joyful abandon. That was the only time that all members of my family danced with each other. It is a memory I will treasure to the grave.

During a brief lull in the proceedings, I went looking for Callum. I found him sitting alone on the back stoop, staring up at the stars. He heard my approach and threw an arm around me, hugging me fiercely to his shoulder. I was slightly taken aback because he was not normally given to displaying signs of affection. I put it down to alcohol, although I could not recall seeing Callum drink more than a couple of glasses of beer. To hide my confusion, I thrust my hand into my pocket and withdrew a small brown paper package.

I worked on weekends helping the local butcher with his deliveries. With one eye on a fine collection of tin soldiers in the window of the toy shop on High Street, I had managed to save a few pennies. When Callum's call to arms arrived, I hurried to the High Street but passed by the toy shop with only a wistful glance at the ranks of gleaming soldiers arrayed behind the glass. I stopped instead a few doors down, at the pawnbroker. Gathering dust in the window was a St Christopher medallion. After a spot of bartering, I managed to persuade the old skinflint who owned the shop to part with the medallion in exchange for my meagre handful of coins. The medallion was tiny, smaller than a ha'penny bit, and was probably cast from some alloy with a heavy tin content. By the time I had finished with the buffing cloth, it shone like silver.

I handed the small package to Callum.

"Got you a present, Cal," I said shyly. As he tore open the paper to reveal a cardboard box, I added, "It's a Saint Christopher. He's the patron saint of travellers, you know. You'll be travelling in the army so he'll protect you. Uh, the chain's a bit girly but you can wear it under your shirt. If you want to . . . wear it, I mean."

Callum carefully removed the medallion and chain from their bed of tissue paper in the small box. He held the medallion in the palm of his hand. It gleamed in the starlight. When Callum looked at me, his eyes glinted.

"Thank you, Johnny. I'll be proud and honoured to wear this."

He wrapped the chain around his neck and fastened the clasp. He clutched the medallion tightly in his fist for a moment before dropping it beneath his shirt collar. He motioned to the lower step and I moved to sit between his knees. Callum's arms came to rest lightly upon my shoulders. A great sense of security enveloped me, untainted by fear. What was there to be afraid of? My brother was going to war, but he would return unscathed, of that I was sure.

"Just look at all those stars," he murmured, cupping my chin in his hand and gently lifting my head.

I gazed skywards. It was an exceptionally clear night; cluster upon cluster of stars winked in the pin-cushion sky and a crescent moon grinned crookedly. There were no neon lights in those days to diminish the night sky's vitality. I sat and stared, entranced.

Callum's voice sounded reverential above my upturned head. "Will you look at them all, Johnny. You couldn't begin to count them, could you?"

Not thinking that he required an answer and not wishing to break the spell of the moment, I remained silent.

"So many of them and so far away," murmured Callum. "They make me feel so small, so worthless . . . so bloody *mortal*. Does it make a scrap of difference to them what the whole human race does, let alone one individual?" He sighed.

I had never heard my brother talk in this manner before. He was usually a man of few words, like Da. I wanted him to continue so I held my peace. When his voice came again it was musing, far away.

"Okay," he said. "So I join the army. I might kill hundreds of Germans and come back a hero. Or I could get killed first day in action. Christ! I could be killed during training. Accidents happen."

He laughed shortly, without humour. "What if I head north tomorrow instead of south and run as far away from this war as I can get? Or I could head west to America. Now there's a thought. Whatever, would my actions make the slightest bit of difference in the greater scheme of things? Would my absence have any effect on the outcome of the war?"

Callum sighed again, a deep shuddering breath. Although I didn't fully understand quite what he was talking about, I realised it was something he had to have out with himself. I could not help him other than to be there to lean on while he deliberated.

The silence stretched into minutes. Just when I was beginning to think that Callum wouldn't speak again, he did. His voice was deep and strong, shorn of doubt.

"Even the most insignificant star adds to the brightness of the sky. There is no choice to make. Pull yourself together, man!"

Callum shook himself and bounded to his feet. Bending forward, he gripped me tightly about the shoulders and whispered into my ear, "Don't we have a party to go to, little brother?"

"Aye, Cal," I replied, relieved that he was back to himself.

"Then what are we waiting for, man?" he grinned, pulling me to my feet and leading me inside.

The following morning was bright and sunny, unlike the mood in our house. We were all up early to take breakfast with Callum. He was the only one who ate heartily. Afterwards he hugged Ma and Morfydd, and shook Da firmly by the hand. He ruffled my hair and winked at me. Bending down, he whispered, "It's up to you to look after Morfydd now, Johnny, until I return home."

Then he hoisted his bag onto his shoulder and strode from the house.

The four of us gathered at the garden gate to watch Callum walk up the street. Our silence was only interrupted by the occasional stifled snuffle from Ma or Morfydd.

Callum reached the end of the road and stopped. He turned and waved once. Then he was gone.

That was the last time I saw Callum alive. At least, in the generally accepted sense.

Grief and Flight

It is said that time is the greatest healer. I beg to differ.

I still bear the anguish of my brother's death, despite what took place in that strange, magical place between worlds I knew as the Meadow. The wounds inflicted by the keen blade of loss have not healed. Years, more than sixty of them, have passed like some great river—sometimes slipping lazily by, more often racing in the surge of a torrent but moving, always moving. Yet tears roll down my stubbly old cheeks as I recall that June day in 1940 as though it happened only yesterday.

I did not amble home from school that warm summer's day with my friends like I normally did, discussing the relative merits of Spitfires and Messerschmitts, and swapping cigarette cards. A dark worm of foreboding had been gnawing at my stomach all afternoon. I ran home.

Bursting into the house, breathless and sweating, I stopped in my tracks.

Ma and Morfydd sat at the dining table, half-drunk cups of tea in front of them. Ma clutched a white handkerchief wrapped around her hand like a bandage. Morfydd held hers to her face as though to stem a nose-bleed. Two pairs of red, swollen eyes turned to me.

I only glanced at their pain-creased faces. My eyes were drawn to the sheet of paper that lay on the table between them. It was beige, a colour I still associate with bad news, and unmistakable: a telegram.

My mind spinning, I stood rooted to the spot. I knew what had happened but dared to hope to be wrong. At last I found my voice.

"Ma?" I croaked.

I stared at her, silently imploring her to tell me that some uncle I didn't even know I had was dead. Or that Callum had been wounded and was recovering in a foreign hospital. I willed her with all my might not to tell me that he had been killed. That did not happen to heroes. They were indestructible.

A tear trickled down Ma's nose and dangled. Ma slowly shook her head and the droplet fell, glinting briefly like a jewel as it plummeted.

"*Ma*!" Now there was urgency and fear in my voice. I had to hear her say the words before I could douse that one lingering spark of hope. Fighting back tears that wanted to spill down my cheeks like some acidic lava flow, I beseeched her to tell me.

"Yes, *cariad*," said Ma, her voice thin and wavering. "The telegram is from the War Office . . . about Callum." She took a deep, shuddering breath. "Your brother's been killed. Killed in action. We don't know any more than that. We—" She broke off as grief consumed her. Morfydd came around the table to comfort her as I backed away, stunned at hearing my worst fear confirmed.

With leaden legs I climbed the stairs to the bedroom that I had shared with Callum. I lay on my bed and let my gaze slide over the shelf holding the few odds and ends that belonged to my brother—an empty tobacco tin, a book about football, a metal comb with some missing teeth. The sight of those scant possessions was the catalyst that brought me out of my shock.

Grief welled to the surface in the form of scalding tears that I was helpless to suppress. I turned onto my stomach, buried my face in the counterpane and rode out the storm.

The contents of the telegram were terse: "Regret inform Pvt

Callum David Andrews killed in action France 30th May 1940."

In one sense the stark wording was a blessing. Unlike many families, we did not have to endure the dreadful uncertainty and false hope brought on by the words, 'Missing in action, presumed dead.'

We had no idea how Callum had met his end. Ma telephoned the War Office and was met by a wall of sympathetic, but singularly unhelpful, silence. It was not until the depths of winter that we discovered what had befallen him.

Britain was by then an island under siege. The Battle of Britain had been raging in the skies above the English Channel and we had come perilously close to losing the war.

The knock on the door came as we gathered around the wireless set that was our main source of news. Da answered the door and returned a few moments later with our visitor. It was a young man of small stature, wearing the uniform of an army private. He limped into the living room and stood facing us, twisting his beige cap between his fingers. The uniform hung loosely off his slight frame as though it had been made for someone two sizes bigger.

"Good evening, Mrs Andrews." His eyes anxiously searched Ma's face as if afraid of rejection. "I'm terribly sorry to disturb you. I'm Arthur Black, Private Arthur Black. I am—was—in the same regiment as your son. . . ."

Ma's expression softened. "You must be Blackie that Callum mentioned in his letters."

We had received three letters from Callum, the last of which had been written in France shortly before he died. He had already seen some action although he barely mentioned it in this the most light-hearted of his letters. I laughed uproariously at Callum's anecdotes, failing to read between the lines the precariousness of his existence. My parents and sister weren't fooled. A look passed between them that spoke silently of grim apprehension. I caught the look and a shadow passed over my heart though I did not know why. I was soon to find out. Within a month of Callum penning that last letter, the innocuous looking beige telegram was delivered to our door.

The soldier nodded at Ma. "Blackie's what everyone calls me. We've all got nicknames. Callum's was Magpie."

Ma smiled sadly. "Yes, I know."

Ma had been most indignant when Callum mentioned his nickname in his first letter. She was only mollified when Callum went on to explain that the name was a reference to Newcastle United, nicknamed the Magpies, and had nothing to do with the pilfering nature of the bird. There was another lad from Tyneside in Callum's regiment who had already been christened the more obvious Geordie.

"Please," said Ma, nodding to a vacant armchair. "Won't you sit down?"

Private Black limped to the chair and sank into it thankfully. He accepted Ma's offer of a cup of tea. While Ma and Morfydd busied themselves in the kitchen, he chatted to Da about the progress of the war.

I was spellbound. I had never been in such close proximity to a soldier in uniform. I knelt on the floor alongside his chair and studied his highly polished boots, the webbed belt and regiment badges with absorbed fascination. He looked down at me.

"You must be John."

I nodded. Blackie smiled and reached down, placing his soft cap upon my head. Delighted, I strutted around the room, marching to an imaginary military band, bringing grins to the faces of Da and Blackie.

Once the tea was finished and the men settled back to smoke—Da his ancient ebony pipe and Blackie a hand-rolled cigarette—Ma went straight to the point.

"Well, Blackie," she said, "was there any particular reason for your visit?"

The jollity drained instantly from Blackie. "I was with Callum in France." He glanced at me with eyes that had become hard and grim. "At the end."

Much to my dismay, I was bundled upstairs to bed at this point. True, it was my bedtime but it wasn't every day that we had such an exciting visitor. My protests fell on deaf ears. Da tucked me into bed and closed the door firmly behind him.

I lay in bed pondering upon life's injustices, particularly to ten-year-olds. Why was Morfydd allowed to remain up? She may have been fifteen but—and this was a big but—she was a girl! How was a mere girl allowed to hear things deemed unsuitable for me? It wasn't fair.

Imagining how Callum had met his end had occupied many a sleepless hour. He must have been killed taking out an enemy machine-gun post single-handedly. Or he had fallen during the daring rescue of some innocent civilians under fire from the Germans. Maybe he had deliberately drawn enemy fire to allow his comrades to escape a trap.

I had to know.

I slipped out of bed and into some warm clothes. Knowing which stairs to avoid, I crept silently downstairs. I gained the living room door and pressed my ear to the keyhole. Although muted, I could make out what was being said within.

Blackie was speaking in his gentle Lancastrian tones.

"...target practice. The Luftwaffe's bullet shattered my kneecap. I was one of the lucky ones. Got brought back to Blighty on a tiny fishing smack. Been in hospital in Essex since."

"Will the army discharge you now, son?" asked Da.

Blackie uttered a short laugh. "Got two weeks' leave, then it's back down south to rejoin the regiment. Or what's left of it after Dunkirk."

Ma snorted. "You can't go back to war. That knee isn't up to it."

"Nah, I'm a'right, Mrs Andrews. It just gives me gyp in this cold weather."

There was a few moments' silence. I moved my eye to the keyhole, poised to flee if anyone approached the door. Blackie was sitting opposite, hunched forward at the edge of his chair. I could not see any of my family and I relaxed. If any of them had risen from their seats, I'd have been able to see them. I heard a muffled voice and hurriedly pressed my ear to the keyhole. Da was talking.

" . . . when Belgium surrendered?"

"We was caught by Jerry and that's no mistake," replied Blackie. "Me and Magpie fought side by side. But it was useless. There was too many. Men were shouting, 'Head for the beaches!' We had to run . . . or die."

"I read in the papers," said Da, "that there were almost a million German troops."

"Yes," sighed Blackie. "And tanks and artillery. The *blitzkrieg* they're calling it."

"Were many men killed?" asked Morfydd.

"Thousands," said Blackie. "We ran, me and Magpie. Ran for our lives. We got split up from the regiment in all the confusion. There was no time to look for the others. Jerry was at our heels. We had to keep moving."

"You headed for Dunkirk?" That was Da, his voice sounding gruffer than normal.

"Yes. We marched all day, running when we could. Jerry was so close we could smell the bastard. Oh, beggin' your pardon, ladies. By nightfall, we could see Dunkirk town ahead. The quickest way to reach it was to cut across a ploughed field. Only trouble was, it had been mined."

In the ensuing silence, I once more peeped through the keyhole. Blackie sat, head bowed, twisting his cap through his fingers. I swapped back to my ear as Ma spoke.

"Go on," she said gently.

"Are you sure? Well, all right." He paused to collect himself. "The field had been mined by our own boys. They knew Jerry would be heading through that way. The usual warning signals was placed round the entrance. But we was knackered . . . it was dark . . . we didn't see 'em." He gave a great sigh. "You can guess the rest."

"No," said Ma. "We have to hear what happened to our son. I know—" She broke off as her voice began to falter. She took a deep breath before continuing. "I know this is hard for you, but you must tell us what happened. Leave nothing out. *We have to know.*"

"Yes, son," said Da. "My wife's right. And I doubt you came all this way not to tell us."

"Yes, sir," sighed Blackie. "I came to tell you what happened. But now that I'm here . . . in front of you . . . it's hard."

"Nevertheless," said Da. His tone brooked no argument.

"All right," said Blackie, resignation clear in his voice.

A knot of dread formed in my stomach. Desperate though I had been to hear what Blackie had to say, now that it came down to it I was terrified. Yet I could not walk away. I was of the same mind as my parents: I had to know.

"We set off through the field," said Blackie. "Magpie was in front. Seeing the town spurred him on and he was always one to take the lead. Then . . . that's when it happened."

In the brief pause, I could hear the faint sound of Morfydd sobbing. My parents were silent. Probably holding their breath.

"There was a loud bang and something struck me head on. I was thrown off my feet. I lay looking up at the sky. I wanted to go to sleep. Then I came to my senses. I got to my knees and saw Magpie. He was lying, sort of crumpled up like, on the ground a few yards away. I crawled over to him."

"He'd stepped on a mine?" asked Da. His self-restraint made his words come out slowly and deliberately.

"Yes," said Blackie. "He was still alive but he was dying. The blast took off his right leg, below the knee."

There was a loud gasp from Ma and Morfydd moaned. I swallowed hard, afraid I might vomit.

"I did what I could," said Blackie. "I stopped the bleeding with my belt but he'd lost too much. The ground was soaked red. I could see the bone. It looked yellow. Magpie was shivering. All I could do was hold him in my arms—" Blackie's breath hitched in his chest and I realised that he was choking back tears.

"I held him tight and he stopped shivering. He was whispering to me, 'Blackie, Blackie' over and over. 'I'm right here, Magpie,' I says to him. 'Take this,' he says. His voice was so weak but urgent too. His hand was by his neck. He was fiddling with something. I reached down and took it from his fingers. It was a small medallion—a St Christopher."

My heart lurched and the first tears escaped to run, hot and stinging, down my cheeks. Now Ma was weeping uncontrollably and Da was breathing so deeply I could hear him in the hallway.

"I felt for the clasp to undo the chain," continued Blackie. "'Just yank it off, man,' whispered Magpie. I did and Magpie closed his fist around mine. He was fading fast. I had to lean close to his mouth to catch what he said next. 'When you get home,' he says, 'return it to my brother. Promise me you will.' 'I promise,' I says. 'What's his name?' 'John,' he whispers. His eyes was fluttering and he looked calm, as though about to drift off to sleep. He wasn't in any pain, Mrs Andrews, I'm sure he wasn't. I thought it was over—his body was relaxing—when he forces his eyes open. 'Blackie,' he says. 'Tell John that I'll keep fighting for him. That I'll always fight for him.' Those was his exact words. Then his eyes closed and . . . and he slipped away."

"Oh my good God," breathed Ma, her words faltering as she struggled for control. "What . . . what happened to his body?"

"I'm so sorry, Mrs Andrews," said Blackie. "I would 'ave taken Magpie with me if I could've managed to carry him. But he was so tall and Jerry was so close—"

"No," said Da. "You couldn't have carried him far. You would have been caught. Did you leave him there?"

"I didn't want to leave any warning for Jerry. I wanted them bastards to go through the field. I dragged Magpie back to the entrance and—" I could hear the reluctance in his voice.

"And?" prompted Da.

Blackie sighed again, a deep, mournful sound. "I pushed him as far as I could under the hedge. Then I went back for his leg and did the same with that. I had no choice, there was no time. I'm sorry. . . ."

"That's all right, son," said Da. His voice was close to cracking. "We're not blaming you. You did what you had to." Da's chair creaked. "You look like you could do with a tot of whisky. God knows, I could."

I had heard enough. Fighting back nausea, I crept back upstairs to bed. The full force of my grief breached my defences as I sank beneath the covers.

So much for my grand delusions that war was a noble and heroic undertaking. Blackie's account of Callum's last moments had opened my eyes to war's brutal realities. It was not 'Bang! You're dead.' Men really died. They didn't just fall down and later get up to go home for tea. Dead people never get up again, I understood that now.

I found it particularly difficult to reconcile myself to the manner of Callum's death. To be killed in flight by a mine laid by your own side—could there be a more inglorious way to die?

Blackie's account shattered my innocence. Never again would I join in those childish war games or fantasise about glory and heroes. That winter night, I took a huge stride towards manhood.

I wept for hours. I wept anew for the death of my brother. I wept at the horror of his destruction. I wept for the passing of my childhood.

The next day, Da took me to one side. If he noticed that my eyes were puffy, he made no mention of it. He told me how Callum had died, although he omitted the more gruesome aspects. As Da finished the tale, he dug into his pocket and withdrew the medallion.

"Here, John," he said. "Your brother wanted you to have this."

I glanced at the St Christopher. Though my vision was blurred, I could see that the clasp on the chain was twisted where Blackie had yanked it from my dying brother's neck. I had to resist a sudden urge to hurl the medallion into the living room fire. It had been meant to protect Callum. But something stayed my hand and I shoved the medallion into my trouser pocket.

If anything positive can be said about Morfydd's death, it is that at least it was an enemy bomb that killed her.

She died in March 1943. We had waved her off from the station the year before, shortly after her seventeenth birthday. My last view of my sister was her mop of dark curls above a face that glowed with excitement at heading for London to take up a junior secretarial post with the Ministry of Defence. She craned out of the window and windmilled her arms frantically as the train rounded a bend and disappeared.

I will never know why she didn't make it to the shelter in time. She was on her way to the underground station when the bomb hit the three-storey building that she was passing. The deadly concrete hail crushed the life from her in an instant.

We received another telegram.

At least this time there was a body to bury.

Ours wasn't the only family to suffer. Almost everyone that I knew lost someone to the war. Many of Callum's peers were killed or maimed, among them Mitch Mahoney. He lost his life on the sands of Africa during the struggle against Rommel. I felt a twinge of sorrow upon hearing of Mitch's death. I had never liked him particularly—he was, after all, a thug and bore a grudge towards Callum—but I always felt that there was more good in Mitch than bad. To use Ma's analogy, Mitch's shade of grey tended towards white rather than black. Moreover, despite his faults, Mitch was from our town and we mourned our own without discrimination.

But tragedy is not only the companion of war. It can strike at any time. And it wasn't finished with us yet.

The end of the Second World War came at last upon a wave of exultation and relief. It took two monstrous acts of destruction to force Japan to its knees but the full horror of the bombs dropped onto Nagasaki and Hiroshima did not hit home until much later. At the time, all we cared about was that the war was finally over.

The end of the war coincided with the end of Da's working life. The cancer lurking in his bowels had started to sap his vitality. Weight fell from him as the malignant cells spread, greedily devouring everything in their path. It is testament to my father's strength of character and constitution that he denied the cancer its ultimate victory for another two years.

That period was extremely painful for Ma and me. Distraught as we had been by the losses of Callum and Morfydd, we were spared having to watch them die before our eyes. There can be few more distressing experiences than watching the life of a loved one slowly being squeezed out while you look on, powerless to intervene.

Ma and I were helpless onlookers to the hardest struggle of Da's life. His spirit remained unbroken to the end but it could not enable his flesh to withstand the onslaught from those murderous, mutant hordes. We watched as his body withered like an unpicked grape on a vine.

Although Ma had plenty of time to come to terms with Da's death, it still tore her apart.

Like most British women of her day, Ma displayed remarkable forbearance and resilience throughout the war years. The deaths of her two eldest children hit her hard; rolling up her sleeves and stiffening her upper lip, she refused to cave in. But Da was the rock upon which Ma's fortitude was founded. As his life ebbed away like sand through an hourglass, her defences crumbled. By the end, Ma had become tearful and fragile, her frail body a canvas upon which her emotions were displayed for all to see.

Weeks after Da's funeral, Ma had not improved. If anything, she was becoming worse, caught in a downward-spiralling vortex of depression. I was shocked by the change in her. She had always been so calm and resolute. It was nearly more than I could bear to see her choked with despair. So when she suggested moving away from the north-east to make a fresh start, I readily agreed.

Ma had an elder sister, Gwen, who I had never met. She lived the life of a spinster in a remote village in Cornwall, having caused some scandal in her God-fearing home village that Ma refused to talk about.

I had seen a photograph of Gwen. The grainy sepia image was of a woman strikingly similar to Ma, although the differences between the two women emphasised the contrast in their fortunes. Where Ma's lips were full and ready to turn into a smile, Gwen's were tightly compressed into a thin line; where Ma's brow was clear, her sister's was creased as if given readily to frowning.

I arrived home to our rented stone terrace from what turned out to be my last day at work as an apprentice bricklayer to find Ma waiting for me, a smile on her lips. Thin and forced it may have been, but it was the first time she had smiled in any fashion for months. She was clutching a telegram. For once, the news was good.

"It's from your Auntie Gwen, John. She says we can stay with her as long as we like. We need to catch a train to Penzance. Be a love and go and buy the tickets, will you?"

As I hurried to the railway station, it began to sink in that we were really going to leave the only home I had ever known. I did not feel as much sorrow at the prospect as I might have anticipated. Since Callum's death, I had become introspective and withdrawn, drifting apart from my friends. Like Ma, I had come to associate Newcastle with suffering and decay. I had never been out of Tyneside and the thought of moving to another part of the country excited me. I knew nothing about Cornwall, other than it was about as far away from Newcastle as it was possible to go without leaving mainland Britain. That snippet of knowledge somehow heightened my excitement. And overriding all other considerations was my concern for my mother. If moving away might restore her equanimity, I was all for it.

When I arrived back home, two one-way tickets to Penzance safely in my pocket, Ma was finalising the sale of our furniture to a local dealer. We needed the money. As Da had not worked for the last two years of his life, we had no savings. We would be leaving with some loose change in Ma's purse and very little else.

No-one waved us off. We had not told any of our friends and neighbours that we were going. We wanted to leave unobtrusively, without any fanfare or farewells that might make our resolution falter. Like two fugitives, we left our home silently before first light and slunk away into the gloom.

We stood on the platform in the early morning drizzle, each of us clutching a bag containing a motley collection of clothes and small personal items. The train emitted grey steamy belches as it hissed to a halt. We settled on board and watched Newcastle recede into the mist.

My mother and I fled—she from the horrors of her immediate past, me from the only life I had known. As we slipped out of Tyneside and headed for the south, I hunched my shoulders and slept.

I dreamed about Callum. He was sitting across the carriage from me, regarding me serenely. He was smiling.

Black Tops

We arrived at our destination in the late afternoon of a warm day in early April 1947. The journey had been long and sometimes arduous. We travelled the last ten miles on the back of a cart that bore the musky odour of animals, bumping along a rutted lane that led to the village. The cart was driven by a cheery old farmer who had regarded us almost with pity when we approached him in the town and asked for directions to Tregeagle.

"You want to go to Tregeagle?" he said in his odd, guttural accent, his bushy eyebrows arched.

"Yes," I replied, trying to keep my voice even. I was tired and dirty, and wanted only to reach my aunt's house as quickly as possible. I glanced at Ma. She offered me a wan smile that was underlain with exhaustion. "Is there a bus we can catch, or perhaps a hansom cab?"

The man's shoulders shook in silent mirth. I gritted my teeth. "A hansom cab?" he grinned. "You won't find no hansom cabs around these parts. And no bus goes to Tregeagle."

Struggling hard now to keep the annoyance from my voice, I asked, "Well, what does go there?"

"There's the postal van in the morning. But you'll be unlikely to get a lift from that grumpy old bugger. Otherwise, there's only the goods van. That delivers once a week. Let me see . . . the next delivery is Wednesday."

I groaned. The man's grin grew wider. I felt like thumping him.

"But you're in luck," he said. "I'm heading that way myself, once I've finished my business in town. I'll be glad to give you a lift. If you don't mind riding on the back of the cart."

I glanced again at Ma. She looked ready to drop. I turned back to the man and, for the first time, returned his grin.

I helped Ma down from the cart. With a wave the farmer went on his way. I fancied that he shook his head from side to side as he pulled off, but it might just have been the motion of the cart.

Ma and I stood in the dusty lane, dirty, dishevelled and bone-tired, and tried to take in our surroundings.

I was a city boy through and through. My playground had been alleyways, disused buildings and street corners. The closest I had ever been to the countryside was the patch of wasteground upon which we played football and that bore as much weeds, junk and ashes from itinerants' fires as it did grass.

I noticed three things simultaneously: the absence of sound, the absence of smell and the presence of colour.

Apart from the fading clip clop of the farmer's horse, there was no noticeable sound at all. Accustomed as I was to roaring and horns of traffic, belching of trains and chimneys, shouting and shrieking of urchins and street vendors, whistling of policeman and factories, and hustle and bustle of thousands of people going about their business, the silence was unnerving.

The stench of the city is almost palpable enough to touch—industrial and domestic smoke, traffic fumes, steam from trains and washhouses, waste from humans and industry—and yet is unnoticed by its inhabitants. Unnoticed, that is, until left behind. Standing uncertainly in that lane, I feared that my nose had stopped working. It hadn't, of course, but it was inhaling fresh country air which possessed no odour that my senses could detect.

The predominant colour of Newcastle had been a sooty, dirty grey. Here, I was surrounded by greenery. Other colours too. Early wild flowers of all hues poked randomly through grass and hedgerow that bordered the lane. White and pink blossom clung in glorious profusion to boughs of trees. The sky was a lightly flecked blue, unsullied by smoke, unobstructed by buildings.

I looked at Ma. Some colour had returned to her cheeks as she turned her head from side to side, her eyes bright. She caught my eye and smiled.

"It's beautiful, John. So colourful, so fresh. It's like this where I come from. It's so easy to forget. . . ."

I grabbed her arm. "Come on. Let's go and find Gwen."

Carrying our bags with our free hands, we walked together into the centre of Tregeagle.

It was little more than a hamlet.

The lane split briefly into two to bound a small oval of rough grass. In the centre of this green stood a dark iron contraption that, at first, I took to be some strange farming implement. Then I realised that I had seen pictures of these very things in books - it was a hand pump for drawing water from the ground. Presumably it had been left in place like a museum piece, a reminder of simpler days gone by.

Facing each other across the green were two rows of buildings that arced into loose approximations of semi-circles. Some stood immediately adjacent to the lane so that anyone leaving them would step out of the front door and onto the lane's pitted surface. Others were set back from the lane with gardens marked by a wall or fence and flagstone paths leading to the doors. The buildings to our right occupied a rise so that they looked slightly down onto the structures opposite. Behind the higher buildings rose densely forested hillside, forming a dark green, almost black, backdrop.

Nearly all the buildings appeared to be dwellings, small tumbledown cottages in the main with ageing thatched roofs. A larger structure to our left was obviously a tavern—a sign swaying gently in the light breeze identified it as *The Smugglers' Reach*—and I could see what looked like a tiny stone church.

I looked around for someone who could direct us to my aunt's house. Pleasant afternoon though it was, there was nobody in sight. I could see no invitingly open windows or doors and no sound of humanity came to my ears. I shivered.

"Let's ask at the pub," I said.

My voice sounded strident in the silence and Ma jumped. Her recently-revived spirits were being dampened by the lack of a welcoming feel about the village. We needed to find my aunt's house so Ma could rest without further ado.

I pushed open the low wooden door of *The Smugglers' Reach* and we entered. My first thought was that the occupants had fallen silent as if Ma and I were a sheriff and deputy entering a saloon full of villains. As my eyes adjusted to the gloomy interior, I realised that the bar had already been silent—there was not a soul in there.

Ma glanced about her, looking panicky, as if fearing we had fetched up in some sort of ghost town. Feeling a touch spooked myself by the emptiness, I strode to the bar and rapped loudly on the pitted oak with my knuckles.

"Hello!" I called. "Anybody home?"

I was rewarded by the sound of shuffling footsteps. A man appeared from a door behind the bar and lumbered forward until he stood the other side of the dark surface from me. I held out my hand in greeting. If he was typical of the inhabitants of Tregeagle, things did not look too promising. He was a large man, probably somewhere in his late thirties. Plain woollen clothes clung to his bulky frame and long ape-like arms hung loosely at his sides. His head was massive, like a prize pumpkin, and lank black hair framed his round face. It is tempting to say that he looked stupid but that would imply that his face bore an expression.

The man's eyes moved slowly down to stare at my outstretched hand, but he made no move to grasp it. Chagrined, but determined not to show it for Ma's sake, I lowered my arm.

"Hello," I said to him. "We're just arrived from Newcastle, you know, in Tyneside. We've come to stay with me Ma's sister Gwen."

At the sound of my voice the man's gaze came back to my face.

"Um, do you know her? My aunt?" I floundered. "Gwen . . . er, Gwen Evans? She lives in a house called Black Tops. Can you tell us where that is? Please?"

At first, nothing. Then, like the sun emerging from behind a slow-moving cloud, a smile appeared on the man's face. While not lending him any aspect that could be described as attractive, it transformed his features from the blankness of a tailor's dummy into something resembling a living person.

He opened his mouth. "She be from Wales be Miss Evans." His accent was coarse but his voice surprisingly gentle for one so big.

"Aye, man, I know. I'm her nephew and this is her sister." I inclined my head towards Ma.

"Wales ain't in Cornwall," he intoned. "Bain't even be in England."

"Do you know where Miss Evans lives?" I asked, struggling not to lose patience.

"Aye. That I do."

I waited expectantly for more. There did not appear to be any. I tried again.

"So, will you tell us where she lives . . . please?"

Comprehension seemed to dawn at last. He shuffled around the bar and towards the door. We followed him outside. He stopped so abruptly I almost blundered into his broad back. He pointed back in the direction we had come.

I saw Aunt Gwen's house immediately. It was the first property on the left when entering the village. We had passed it in the cart but must have been too engrossed with the first sight of our new habitat to take in details. It was large compared to the neighbouring cottages, of two storeys, set back from the road. I could clearly make out the upper storey and roof above the thatch of the adjacent cottage and I knew that I was looking at Black Tops. The roof of my aunt's house was clad in slate. The slate was black, so black that it could have been tar.

I turned to thank the man for his help but only caught a glimpse of his woolly jerkin as he disappeared through the door of the pub. I called out our gratitude and looked at Ma. She was staring at the black roof, her eyes gleaming. Hoisting my bag onto my right shoulder, I held out my left arm.

"Shall we?" I asked.

Ma giggled like a young girl and took my arm.

"Well," I mused, "we've come the length of England to reach this place. We've travelled by rail, by bus and by cart. We're tired, we're dirty and we're hungry. And who's the only person to greet us? Why, the Village Idiot!"

Ma glanced at me, trying to keep a straight face. It was no good. Within seconds, we were both laughing like loons.

Black Tops was approached through a peeling iron gate set into a drystone wall over which roses rambled. A flagstone path, cracked and uneven, led to the weathered front door between blossom-crowned fruit trees and ranks and files of fruit canes and bushes.

The house was imposing, constructed from the same rough stones that formed the boundary wall. The walls bore the flaking evidence of some long ago whitewashing.

I pushed open the creaking gate and we picked our way up the path to the front door. I cannot recall that I felt any sense of foreboding as I prepared to enter my aunt's home. Certainly I was nervous about meeting Ma's sister but I felt no apprehension about the house itself.

An older version of Ma appeared in answer to my knock. As she recognised Ma, a delighted grin split her face and her eyes brimmed with tears that cascaded merrily down her plump cheeks. I could see immediately that the photograph Ma had shown me did Gwen no favours. Her lips *were* thinner than my mother's, her brow more creased, but she was far less harsh, less grim in person than the grainy photograph had suggested.

"*Cariad!*" she exclaimed. "*Duw!* It's wonderful to see you, girl!" She stepped out of the doorway and she and Ma fell into each other's arms.

At last they drew apart. "It's wonderful to see you too, Gwen," said Ma. "It's been far too long." She turned to me. "Gwen, I'd like you to meet my son John."

I stepped forward, my hand extended politely. "Hello, Auntie Gwen. Pleased to meet you."

For the second time that afternoon, my outstretched hand was ignored. Gwen threw her arms around me in a surprisingly strong bear hug. I could not help but inhale her odour of lavender and balsam. She even smelled like Ma.

She pulled away and looked intently up at me. "Gosh! You're the image of your father." She clapped her hands. "You two must be famished after such a long trip. Let's go and eat. Come in, come in."

We followed her inside and I closed the front door behind me, shutting out the daylight. The hall was narrow and darkly panelled, illuminated by an oil-lamp that stood on a small table at the foot of a staircase that rose into blackness.

Gwen led us beyond the gloom of the hall, through a heavy door into the kitchen. A large window looked out over the back garden and the fields and woods beyond, letting in sunlight that bathed the room in a warm glow. My glance took in the huge oil lamp that hung from a hook affixed to the middle beam in the ceiling and the cast iron range that occupied one wall.

"Er, Cornwall does have electricity, doesn't it?"

Gwen laughed. "Yes, love, Cornwall has electricity. Unfortunately, the mains haven't yet found their way to Tregeagle. Don't look so worried; you'll get used to it."

I was soon to discover that mains gas had not yet reached Tregeagle either. Heat was provided by log and coal fires, lit in every room during the winter. Cooking was carried out over log-burning stoves and ranges like Gwen's. Accustomed as I was to the conveniences and facilities of a modern city, I felt a weird sense of disassociation, as if I had stepped back in time to a bygone age in a forgotten world.

The means by which food was cooked may have been antiquated but the food produced by Gwen employing those means was the most wonderful I have ever tasted. Ma and I were ravenous and we tucked into the meal that Gwen placed before us as though we hadn't eaten for weeks. In Ma's case, that was almost true; at least, she had not eaten properly since it became obvious that Da had a very short time left, and that had been many weeks before. We ate like horses.

After dinner and as night fell, we remained at the table and chatted. I watched Ma as she nattered. Her eyes shone brightly in the flickering light of the lamp and she smiled often. The colour gradually returned to her cheeks.

I crawled into bed very early that night, exhausted, hundreds of miles from the only home I had ever known, but content.

The feeling of contentment with which I had retired to bed on our first night did not last long. It was soon replaced by boredom. What on earth did the inhabitants of Tregeagle do for entertainment? Very little as far as I could tell.

Of course, there were places to explore. I started with the back garden, which was large and verdant compared to the gardens I was used to. Gwen had a couple of surprises in her back garden. In a muddy pen she kept two pigs and, nearby, some chickens and two surly geese. I was delighted that she kept pets. It was only when I enquired of their names did I realise that they served a more fundamental purpose than providing companionship to an elderly lady living alone.

"Names? Don't be *twp*. You don't give names to animals that will be on your dinner plate before the year is out." Gwen chuckled, her ample backside rolling with mirth as she went to find Ma to share the joke.

I could understand her lack of sentiment. I could not imagine myself having the courage to slit a pig's throat or wring a bird's neck, especially if I had reared and nurtured the creature. But if I was going to help feed and muck-out the pigs, I had to call them something. So I christened them Bangers and Mash and soon Ma too was calling them by their new names. They remained as just the pigs to Gwen.

One evening I had the chance to ask my aunt the question that had been smouldering in my mind like a cinder since the day we arrived. Ma had retired early with a slight head cold. Gwen and I sat at the kitchen table.

"Auntie Gwen, can I ask you a question?"

"Of course, love. Whether I can answer it is another matter."

"Well, you said when you first saw me that I looked like my father. When did you meet him?"

She looked at me sharply. "You're smart, lad, I'll give you that. Your mother never noticed my slip." She was quiet, looking down at her hands that fidgeted with her mug on the table. Then she lifted her head and I was surprised at her stern expression.

"Your mother has never shown me a photograph of your father and, no, I have never met him. I have seen him though. Once."

I frowned, not understanding.

"Look, love," she said. "You mustn't repeat to your Ma what I am about to tell you. Promise?"

I nodded.

"Good. I couldn't bear it if your Ma knew this sorry tale."

She took a deep breath before continuing. "I left home under a cloud when I was twenty-four. My parents sent me away in disgrace and I hated them for it. At least, that's what I convinced myself. What I'd done was pretty bad in them days, although I didn't do it on purpose. I was young and impressionable and he was so handsome. He was also married, see, though I didn't know it until too late.

"Still, I thought my parents would forgive me, or at least my Mam. I was, after all, their eldest child. They had loved me longer than their other kids. But . . . no. It was against the teachings of the Chapel see, *cariad*. That bloody preacher with his hellfire and brimstone. He put the fear of God into people. And my father had always been easily led. He was so gullible. I think he honestly believed that some terrible retribution would come down upon the family if he didn't send me away. His fear of God was certainly stronger than his love for his daughter. The weak bastard!"

Gwen paused to collect her thoughts. I suspected that she had not spoken about these things for a very long time, if ever.

"The worst thing," said Gwen, "was the look in Mam's eyes as Dad spoke the words that would banish me from home. She didn't want me to go but she was too afraid to stand up to him. What a pair—both too blinded by fear to do what was right. *He* took advantage of me. *He* should have been the one to be sent away in disgrace. I might have been in my twenties, but I was still only a kid. I knew nothing.

"Anyway, I left the village, I left Wales. I had done what had to be done and then wandered for a few years, from place to place, job to job. I came down here just after the end of the Great War and here I've been ever since.

"I wrote home, out of a sense of duty more than anything, to let them know that I was alive. I wanted them to feel guilty too. When Mam wrote back almost begging me to go home, for a moment I was tempted. But I had been too hurt by their rejection. If they had come here and asked me in person . . . if Dad had apologised, I might have gone back with them. But he was too pigheaded and I heard nothing further from them.

"I stayed in touch with your mother though. We had always been close. She sent me a telegram when Mam died. But I couldn't go to the funeral. I still felt too much bitterness towards Dad. If I had gone, I would have caused a scene, I know I would have. It was better for everyone that I stayed away. I think your Ma understood."

She grimaced as if she were expelling a nasty taste from her mouth. In a sense, that is precisely what she was doing.

"Dad lasted another three years on his own. Emphysema did for him—his days down the pit caught up with him in the end.

"Your mother sent me another telegram. This time I did go to the funeral, though I told no-one, not even your Ma, of my plans. I returned to Wales for the first and only time. I arrived early and went straight to the cemetery. When I saw the funeral cortege approaching, I lost my nerve and hid behind some fir trees that screened the graveyard from the slag heaps. I watched my father lowered into the ground, peering through branches like a fugitive.

"*That* is when I saw your father. He stood with his arm around your mother, comforting her with his strength and love. I only watched him for a short time, but I could tell that he was a good man who doted on my little sister. It's little wonder that she fell apart when he died.

"Did I say *little* sister? Not any more she wasn't. A fine figure of a woman she had become. I longed to rush out and throw my arms around her. But something held me back. Perhaps it was the sight of relatives and friends that I had not seen in years that cowed me. More likely it was the sense that I was intruding that made me stay hidden. That place was my home, is still my home in my heart of hearts, but I felt like a stranger. That's a terrible feeling. It hardened my attitude towards my father even more.

"I remained crouched behind those trees for the next two hours. I was bursting for a pee but I couldn't come out until the grave diggers had finished their work. I vaguely recognised one of them and I didn't want word to reach your Ma that I had been there. To be honest, I was ashamed—ashamed that I was afraid to show myself, but more too. The worst part was the old feeling of disgrace that your grandfather had etched onto my soul returned with a vengeance. I thought I had exorcised that particular ghost, but I was wrong, oh so wrong. Then I hated him. Truly hated him.

"When at last the men had gone, I crept out of my hiding place and stood over the mound of earth. I said goodbye to my father. It wasn't a fond farewell." She gave a short laugh, shorn of humour.

"It was almost dark by then. I must have been out of my senses. Do you know what I did John? I hitched up my skirt, squatted and relieved myself on his grave. I pissed on my dead father."

I had no idea what to say so I said nothing.

"He had his revenge though, my father. No sooner had I arrived back here than he came to haunt me. He's haunted me ever since."

Local Relations

The days and weeks slipped by slowly. April turned unnoticed into May. There was no sense of time in Tregeagle. We ate when we were hungry, slept when it was dark, awoke when it was light. Gwen kept a couple of clocks about the house that she wound religiously, but more out of habit than necessity.

Ma's mental health improved daily. She still grieved for Da and her children, of course, but in a natural, healthier sort of way.

There were no paid jobs in the village so I busied myself helping Gwen. I fed the poultry, mucked out the pigs, repaired the drystone garden wall where it was toppling through neglect. When the showery spring weather permitted, I stripped the exterior walls of the house of its peeling whitewash. It looked a great deal better with the natural Cornish stone showing in place of the flaking yellow lime.

One of my daily chores was to collect water each morning from the centre of the village. The hand pump that I had noticed on our arrival at Tregeagle and had assumed to be a museum piece was in fact entirely functional. As with electricity and gas, mains water had not yet found its way to the village. It was like living in the Dark Ages. Every household in the village drew its water from the pump. Remote as the village was, its inhabitants would be in serious trouble if ever the well that fed the pump ran dry.

Each morning before breakfast, I'd stroll out to the village green, jauntily swinging Gwen's iron pail by my side. Placing the pail beneath the spout, I grabbed the smooth pump handle with both hands and jerked it up and down until, with a gurgle and gush, ice cold water came spurting from the spout. It wouldn't take long to fill the pail and then would begin the return journey.

This was neither jaunty nor a stroll. More like a shambling lurch, struggling to prevent water sloshing over the sides of the pail. More than once in those first days I had to return to the pump for more water as I'd lost so much on the return journey. But I soon became proficient in walking with short strides, back and arms straight, keeping the bucket stable and it was only for a week or two that my arms and shoulders whined and grumbled at the demands fetching water placed upon them.

There was one peculiar aspect of my daily trip to the pump. Although each household in the village had to perform the same daily ritual to fetch their water, not once did I meet another villager at or on the way to or from the pump. Had this been Newcastle, the green would have been a bustling hive of activity and it would probably have taken three times longer to fetch the water, what with having to stop for a chat or a kickabout or having to sort out some minor act of vandalism to the pump.

I put it down to the natural reserve of country folk. Very private, very shy were the good people of Tregeagle.

There was another very curious thing about the village. My explorations had grown gradually more wide-ranging, taking in the surrounding countryside and reaching the rugged coastline. It was only upon returning to the village from these expeditions that I noticed the difference. Everywhere I ventured in the woods and fields around Tregeagle, and more so as I neared the sea, I heard the calls, chatterings, whoops and whistles of birds. I noticed these sounds as a country dweller would notice the sounds of traffic in a city. However, within the boundaries of the village I couldn't hear as much as the chirp of a sparrow.

When I first noticed the absence of bird song in the village, I thought I must be imagining things and put it to the test. I stood very still in the back garden of Black Tops and listened. All I could hear were the soft clucks of Gwen's chickens and the occasional grunt from Bangers and Mash. I walked around the village, to the green and along the lanes that passed in front of the cottages, stopping now and then to listen intently. Still no bird song.

It was only when I had walked a few hundred yards along the lane that led out of the village that the air became alive with the cooing of wood pigeons, the cawing of crows and the scolding of jackdaws.

Back to the village and nothing—absolute feathery silence.

The wall that bounded Gwen's rear garden had a stile built into it. On the other side of the stile was a buttercup-studded meadow that sloped gently away from Black Tops to a wood. A path led through the wood to moorland which in turn led to the coast, some three miles or so from the house.

In the meadow, about twenty yards beyond the stile, was a wide indentation partially covered with water that formed a murky pond. Wild grass and buttercups gave way to reeds that grew at the water's edge. Gnats and the occasional dragonfly frequented the surface of water the colour of beef broth. I was no expert on pond life but I expected to find a few newts or frogs inhabiting the broth that perhaps was three feet at its deepest.

I once walked out to the pond armed with an empty jam jar and a length of twine. I attached the string securely to the neck of the jar and cast it into the centre of the pond. When I pulled the jar out, it contained nothing but silty water. I repeated the process in various spots with the same results—no frogs, no spawn, no newts, no water beetles, no larvae. Dragging the jar across the bottom yielded nothing except oozing mud. The pond seemed devoid of life.

Yet, during the hour or so that I stood at its banks, casting the jar into the water and hauling it back out, it felt as though eyes were watching me. More than once, I turned around sharply, certain there was someone standing behind me but there was no-one there.

When I gave up and walked back through the field to Black Tops, I glanced back once or twice more. There was still nobody there but the feeling of being watched persisted until I had climbed the stile and stood in the back garden.

Except it wasn't exactly a sensation of being watched; more one of being *considered.*

I have probably made Tregeagle out to be some sort of ghost village, but of course it was not really like that. True, the inhabitants did keep themselves to themselves and I didn't meet everyone who lived there during our stay. I did meet some, though.

There was one encounter with the locals that particularly bears repeating since it represented a turning point in Ma's recovery from the veil of despondency that had hung around her like a ragged shroud since Da's death.

It was the day that I went to the village shop to buy goods for Gwen.

Many inhabitants of Tregeagle were largely self-sufficient. People kept pigs, chickens, geese, goats; they grew potatoes, beans, cabbages, carrots and lots more; they nurtured apple, plum and pear trees. Gwen grew raspberries, strawberries and rhubarb in the back garden of Black Tops. The mild Cornish climate was ideal for horticulture. I can still recall the patch of rhubarb ripening in the sun, a small army of umbrella-like canopies shivering in the late summer breezes.

One family kept a small flock of sheep in the field behind their cottage. They didn't know who actually owned the field but nobody ever objected to the sheep grazing there and the flock provided mutton and wool for the village. Another family kept bees that produced runny, sticky honey that Gwen used as a sugar substitute in her cooking.

Goods like sugar were not freely available, even in the main towns.

Britain was toiling under the strictures of rationing and would be well into the 1950s.

A system of bartering was still prevalent in Tregeagle. Gwen exchanged pork products—ham, bacon, sausages—goose and chicken eggs and surplus fruit for produce like honey and wool. A huge walk-in larder led off from Gwen's kitchen, walls three feet thick to keep the interior cool. Sides of bacon and ham hung curing from hooks in a beam in the ceiling. Occasionally, a haunch of venison or pheasant would join them, courtesy of a barter with a resident whose activities appeared to include poaching from a wealthy landowner's estates that lay to the north of the village beyond the forest.

The system seemed to work. Certainly, Gwen was able to absorb the demands of two extra mouths to feed without any noticeable hardship.

Gwen couldn't barter or produce everything we needed. Oil for the lamps, cotton, tools, some items of clothing, shoes and other necessities like flour had to be purchased from the nearest town or from the village shop. A delivery van came rattling down the lane from town once a week to restock the shop. Dairy produce and beef were also sold in the shop but were provided by the farm that was situated up the lane in the other direction from town. The farm was owned by the man who had given Ma and me a lift to the village upon our arrival from Newcastle.

Bangers and Mash were the main sources of Gwen's income. Breeding pigs, they were. Gwen kept one or two offspring from each litter to fatten and slaughter. The rest she sold at the market in town and was usually able to make sufficient profit to last her until the next litter. Although Mash had become pregnant towards the end of our stay in Tregeagle, I wasn't witness to any slaughtering or piglet-selling, for which I was grateful. Not that I was squeamish, but I think it might have been a bit of a blow to my city-boy sensibilities to have been brought into such close contact with the realities of self-sufficient country life.

The village shop was on the far side of the green from Black Tops, a few doors away from *The Smuggler's Reach*. I strolled through the village one morning early in June, a clutch of coins jangling in my pocket. It was a bright day, the sun already warm in a clear sky, promising a fine summer to come.

The shop did not look particularly welcoming. It was one storey with a low thatched roof in need of attention. The faded wooden door was set into the centre of the stone walls with two sets of small-paned windows to either side. I put my face to one. The glass was grimy and I could see nothing within except the suggestion of vague, shadowy shapes.

My cheeriness slightly dampened, I pushed the door open and entered.

A harsh jangling sounded from somewhere above my head. As the door swung closed behind me, I stood for a moment, allowing my eyes to adjust to the gloom.

The shop obviously catered for every requirement that the villagers could not supply themselves. It was a grocer, delicatessen, tailor, milliner, newsagent, tobacconist, confectioner and hardware shop all under one roof. Sacks of grain and flour filled one corner. Bales of cotton and swathes of cloth occupied another. Motes of dust swirled in the weak sunlight that the grime on the windows allowed in.

Gardening implements, iron pails and a variety of tools took up space here and there, or hung from hooks attached to low beams beneath the roof. A rack of shelves took up one wall, cluttered with tins of fruit, condensed milk, tea leaves, luncheon meat and sardines. Another shelf held a variety of hats—flat caps, trilbies, boaters, ladies' hats—while others contained folded chunky jumpers, roughspun shirts and trousers, tweed jackets, long skirts. Yet another shelf displayed footwear, from clumsy-looking gum boots to house slippers.

There was more, much more. I had never seen such a wide range of merchandise within one space.

At the back of the shop was a darkly-stained wooden counter that ran the whole width of the building. It looked like a bar without beer handles. Behind the counter was more floor-to-ceiling shelving, crammed with boxes of nails, tins of tobacco, cans of oil and paraffin, and jars of liquorice, aniseed balls and gobstoppers.

And the smells . . . rubbery, sugary, oily, acridity, all jostling for attention in my overworked nostrils.

I must have stood there for minutes, staring round in wonder, before I noticed that I wasn't alone.

Standing at the back of the shop, behind the counter, was a small, shrewish woman in her late fifties. She stared intently at me through wire-framed spectacles. Standing this side of the counter was a customer. He had turned to face my way and was also staring intently at me. He was hunched and gnarled like an ancient oak and must have been in or near his seventies, a ripe old age in those days. Neither he nor the shopkeeper spoke or acknowledged my presence in any way, other than the stares.

I nodded briefly in their direction and moved around the shop. The back of my head itched under their regard, but I was determined not to be intimidated—I had been brought up in the rough-and-tumble world of Tyneside; I could withstand a little staring from two old folk. I worked my way among the array of wares, examining things closely, whether I was interested in them or not.

There was a small rack of newspapers, most only a few days old. I can still, well over half a century later, remember the subjects of the stories on the front page of *The Times*: the proposed partitioning of India and the arrest of wives of various Nazis, including Goering's. Strange what things stick in the memory.

The newspaper rack fascinated me as it provided my first link to the outside world since we had arrived in the village. Gwen did not possess the one thing that was as indispensable then as televisions are now: a wireless. I missed the music programmes that my family used to gather round our wireless set to enjoy and I missed the nightly news broadcasts by the BBC's World Service. I knew that Ma did too. She took to calling into the shop once a week to scan the newspaper headlines. She didn't buy one though; that was a luxury we couldn't afford.

I particularly missed news about my beloved Newcastle United—how they were faring in the league, news about player transfers or injuries and so on. Fortunately, there hadn't been much of the season left when we had left the city as otherwise I don't know how I would have coped with the isolation.

So engrossed did I become in the sports section of *The Times* that I had forgotten about the couple watching me. When I looked up at last, they were both still staring at me.

Returning the newspaper to the rack, I cleared my throat and strode to the counter. I addressed the shopkeeper in what I hoped was an assertive, though friendly, voice.

"Hello there. I'm John Andrews. I'm staying at Black Tops with me Aunt Gwen. Me Ma's staying too. They're sisters, see."

The woman continued to stare at me. Her hair was wound up into the sort of tight bun that I associate with strict school ma'ams. I wondered whether she was waiting for more.

"We're from Newcastle originally," I said. "You know, Tyneside."

As she continued to stare at me, saying nothing, I felt a sense of déjà vu. This was exactly how my conversation with the man in the pub had started.

I glanced to my right. The customer was still staring at me too. His mouth was open, revealing pink gums as toothless as a newborn baby's. Now that I was closer, I could see that his eyes were milky, pupils large and swimming beneath a filmy shroud. I could hear his breathing, ragged and rattling in his chest.

I looked away and back to the shopkeeper's stony silence. At last she broke it.

"Do—you—want—to—buy—something?" She spoke slowly, enunciating each word carefully as some people do when they address a foreigner.

"Yes—please," I replied, unable to resist talking in the same fashion.

We regarded each other in silence for a few more moments.

"I'll just finish serving Joe," she said in what I assumed was her normal mode of speaking.

I nodded, thinking better of mentioning that she'd had time to serve Joe ten times over instead of following my every movement.

As she turned back to Joe and, blessedly, he turned his creepy eyes back to her, I collected the things Gwen had sent me to buy. They weren't many. A tin of tea leaves, a two-pound bag of flour and a reel of white cotton. I carried them back to the counter.

Joe was just turning away from the counter, paper bag of purchases clutched to his thin chest in one hand, the other clutching a walking stick as worn and gnarled as he was. I smiled at him. While he had been unable to tear his watery gaze away from me only moments before, now he didn't seem capable of so much as glancing at me. He shuffled past and was gone.

The woman placed my purchases into a paper bag.

"Don't mind old Joe," she said, handing the bag to me. "He doesn't like strangers." I handed over some coins. As she passed me the change, she added, "Can't say that I do either."

She smirked.

About to turn away and leave, I paused.

"Well, there's none stranger than the folk around here," I said, having the satisfaction of seeing her lips purse into a tight crease.

I turned and walked from the shop, my head held high.

Outside, I could see Joe making his way across the green. I half considered running over and kicking away his walking stick, but settled for returning to Black Tops, thinking dark thoughts.

Ma and Gwen were sitting in the kitchen. Judging from the delicious aroma, they had been busy baking bread with the last of the flour.

I handed the bag and change to Gwen. I must still have been looking thoughtful because she asked me what was wrong.

"Oh, nothing," I said. "Just that woman who runs the shop. And some old bloke, a customer. Not very welcoming, shall we say."

"Don't go paying any attention to that old sourpuss," said Gwen. "But, tell us what exactly happened."

I told them. As I did, I noticed a look come into Gwen's eyes that I had seen before. Ma had the same look when she was on the warpath. I glanced at her: she wore it too.

"No harm done," I said hurriedly, but it was too late.

"I'll just get my hat," said Ma and strode belligerently to the hat stand in the hall.

I groaned. Ma always wore her hat into battle. She strode back into the kitchen, hat on head. She looked at her sister.

"Right?" said Ma.

"Right!" said Gwen.

Out they marched like two pocket battleships heading for war.

I felt it might be wise if I followed them. So I trailed along in their wake and peered through the dirty glass window after the shop door had swung shut behind them. Ma and Gwen marched side by side to the counter. The backs of their heads bobbed as they gesticulated at the shopkeeper. I could not make out her expression in the gloom, or hear what Ma and Gwen were saying, but doubted that either was pretty.

They emerged after a few minutes, backs straight, chins thrusting. As we walked away from the shop, they began to giggle like naughty schoolgirls.

"Did you see her face," said Gwen, "when you told her that the Welsh wouldn't take being pushed around lying down? She couldn't work that one out."

"And," said Ma, "when you said '*Twll dyn pob Saes*', she didn't know whether you were insulting her or apologising. . . ." They broke off into hoots of laughter, doubled over and holding weakly onto each other.

"What does that Welsh phrase mean?" I asked, when they had recovered their composure somewhat.

"Can't tell you, love," said Ma. "You've too much English in you."

This set them off again. I watched the tears of mirth running down their cheeks, feeling slightly miffed.

"Tell you what," said Gwen at last. "I've a couple of bottles of home-made elderflower wine in the pantry. Let's get stuck into them."

We supped the wine from clay mugs. It went straight to our heads. We drank and chatted long into the evening, by unspoken consent only speaking of happy times.

I watched Ma as she recounted tales of Callum and Morfydd and me during our childhood, and of Da during their courting days. She listened raptly to Gwen's stories of childhood in the Welsh village and giggled at my occasional tales of scrapes I had got myself into in Newcastle.

Tears occasionally welled from her eyes when Callum or Morfydd or Da were mentioned, but she smiled sadly and absentmindedly brushed them away. There was no sign of the awful despair into which she had fallen following Da's demise. I believed that she had pulled through the dark times and was out on the other side, where the grief still existed but was somehow more natural and bearable.

I was right, too. I never had cause to fear for Ma's mental health again.

Pity I couldn't say the same about my own. I was shortly to fear that I was losing my mind: right about the time that I started meeting my dead brother.

The Meadow

The dreams—if that is what they were—started in June. Unlike most dreams that begin to fade upon awakening like dispersing mist, I can still remember them with vivid clarity, as easily as I can recall events that occurred during my waking hours.

The setting for the dreams was always the same. A field. It grew with ankle-deep soft grass dotted with creamy yellow buttercups and snowy white daisies. The field stretched away in every direction as far as the eye could see to a horizon that shimmered like a desert.

Each dream started in exactly the same way. I would snap out of the deep void of sleep into full awareness, as abruptly as though someone had emptied a bucket of icy water over my sleeping form. I would find myself lying on my stomach in the Meadow, as I came to think of it. It was always the middle of a bright day. If I looked up, I had to clench my eyes against the glare of the sun that beamed from a sky so brilliantly and uniformly blue it looked as if it had been coloured by a child.

On the first occasion that I awoke in the Meadow I lay still for a few moments, luxuriating in the soft embrace of the grass. The sun felt deliciously warm on my back, while a light breeze made the grass sway and cooled me. I plucked a buttercup and held it to my nose. I could smell summer and freshness and vitality. I knew that I was asleep and this was some sort of dream but I have never experienced such vivid, lifelike dreams before or since as I experienced that summer in the Meadow.

As I breathed in the flower's scent, a shadow fell across me and I glanced up. There stood a young man. It was Callum.

He looked the same as when I had last seen him on the morning he had left us to join the army. He stood relaxed, smiling gently down at me. The breeze ruffled his hair just as it had that evening as Callum stood poised waiting for Mitch Mahoney to make his move.

A warm glow settled over me, a calmness that emanated from my brother. I felt no fear as I rose slowly to my feet, unable to take my eyes off him.

"Are you looking after Ma, Johnny?"

It took me a moment—if such things as moments existed in the Meadow—to realise that he had spoken.

"Aye, Cal," was about as much as I could say. That old feeling of tongue-tied hero worship was back.

I dropped my gaze, shyness overcoming wonder. When I looked back up, he had gone. His feet had left imprints in the grass—Callum was not an insubstantial wraith in that place—but there was no sign of footprints leading to or from the spot where he had stood. I felt no sense of loss at his disappearance; somehow I knew that I would see him again.

When I awoke that morning, I could remember the dream clearly, and still can. The warm glow that had come from Callum nestled in my stomach like a good meal. I lay in bed, replaying the dream over and over. I could still smell the buttercup, still see the frayed collar of the faded blue shirt that Callum had been wearing, still taste the blade of grass that I had absent-mindedly chewed as I lay in the Meadow, still feel the warmth of the sun on my back.

I checked myself for signs that it hadn't been a dream—a sliver of grass caught in my teeth, stains or scents on my fingers. But of course there were none. My body hadn't left the bed all night.

My next visit to the Meadow occurred about a week later. That was the pattern: roughly one week between each visit, until the last one in early August. Ten in all. Each one still as vivid in my mind as though they happened yesterday.

The first few visits, probably the first three or four, were very similar. Each time I came to awareness in the Meadow, I'd lie in the sun and wait for Callum. I knew he had arrived when his shadow fell across me. I'd bound to my feet and rush to hug him.

The first time I felt a slight apprehension that I would pass straight through him. But he was solid and hugged me back. His embrace was warm and real. He even smelled as I remembered: of the carbolic soap of my childhood and woody smokiness from the kitchen fire. The only jarring sensation to my recollection of Callum was that the proportions were wrong. If Callum had hugged me when I'd last seen him alive, my face would have been pressed against his ribcage. But Callum had remained eighteen and would be eighteen for ever. I was now only a year younger. Although I would never grow to surpass him in height, I had filled out, grown broader than him, and I stood only an inch or two shorter so that my face comfortably cleared his shoulder as we hugged.

As I pulled back from that first embrace, I looked into his eyes. They were still the same shade of green, suggesting good-nature and kindness, and glinted like the tip of a wave when he smiled. But there were changes. They seemed to be more profound, contain more depth than before, as though their owner had undergone fundamentally altering experiences. I guess he had. Death for one.

Those meetings would pass with us lounging on the grass, chatting about old times; about our friends, old stomping grounds, our family. He seemed to understand that Morfydd and Da had died, but silenced me with a gentle shake of his head if I started to mention them in terms that confirmed their deaths. I dared not approach, even obscurely, Callum's own death, at least not during those first few meetings. So we chatted as though he and Da and Morfydd were still alive and we lived back in Newcastle and I was still ten.

We passed what felt like hours in this manner, but the weather never changed, the sun's position high overhead never altered, the breeze remained steady and I never felt hunger, thirst or the need to urinate.

And of course they were just dreams. Glaringly vivid, but just dreams. And yet . . .

The following day, I would feel exhausted. Black bags like bruises beneath my eyes; dry, spitless mouth; the occasional ache in back or leg as though having lain in one position for too long. In fact, I'd feel precisely as I would have expected to feel if I'd spent all night lying in a field talking.

Ma often remarked on my appearance during breakfast in the mornings following a visit to the Meadow, but I just shrugged it off as a bad night's sleep. Since they only occurred once a week, she never pursued it.

Just as well. I was entertaining serious doubts about my sanity but the last thing I wanted to do was burden Ma with fresh worries. Now that she had emerged from the depths of her despair, I didn't want anything to risk plunging her back into the pit.

And there were no other symptoms of insanity on my part. I did not experience any hallucinations during my waking hours, at least not then. I felt no urges to rip all my clothes off and tie a petunia to my manhood or howl at the moon or quack like a duck. Apart from the night-time visits to the Meadow, I felt perfectly normal.

So I quickly came to accept the dreams as an unlooked-for opportunity to spend time with my older brother. And if they were merely a figment of my imagination, then it was an imagination to revel in. I stopped questioning the dreams' reality and my sanity and simply determined to enjoy them while they lasted.

Then they began to change.

As soon as Callum appeared, I sensed that something had altered. He sat on the grass opposite me, cross-legged, back straight. Face expressionless.

"Cal?" I said gently. "What's wrong?"

After a long pause, he said, "We can't carry on meeting like we have been, Johnny." His words were spoken in that soft, unassuming way that he'd always had, but they dismayed me.

"Why?" I asked. "What's happened?"

"I'm beginning to understand things better. There are reasons why we are permitted to meet like this."

"What reasons? What do you mean, 'permitted'?" I had nothing but questions to which I didn't really want to know the answers.

Callum sighed. "I don't understand enough yet. But I know that I'm no longer part of your world . . . I'm dead there, aren't I?"

"You died seven years ago, Cal." I couldn't keep the sorrow from my voice.

"Seven years? That would have meant something to me once. There is no time where I come from."

"Where do you come from?" It seemed that the taboo on discussing awkward topics had been swept away.

He shrugged his shoulders. "The others call it Darkland." He uttered a short, humourless laugh. "Very apt."

"Others?"

"Oh, there are lots of others. Da and Morfydd aren't among them though. They passed straight through."

"Da and Morfydd . . . you know about them? That . . . that they're dead?"

"Yes."

"Did you see them? Were they happy?"

"Yes. I saw them. Morfydd first. Then Da. They looked at peace."

"Where have they gone, Cal? Why aren't you with them?"

"I don't know where they've gone. Nobody knows what lies beyond Darkland. Wherever or whatever it is, I'll go there too, but not until—"

"Until?" I prompted.

"Look, John. . . ." His eyes narrowed. For the first time in the Meadow, I felt uneasy. A little afraid. "I have some reason for being in Darkland. Some purpose holds me there and I can't move on until I've fulfilled that purpose." He held up a hand to forestall my next question. "It hasn't yet been revealed to me. All I know so far is that it has something to do with you."

"*Me?* What—"

Callum shook his head, almost impatiently. "I don't know, but I'll find out. Until I've done whatever it is, I can't pass on." There was a note of regret in his voice. "I belong with Da and Morfydd now, not here with you."

That stung me but I tried to hide it.

"Are we in Darkland now, Cal?"

He smiled, but only with his lips. His eyes held sorrow.

"No," he said. "That place we used to live. . . ."

"Newcastle."

"Yeah, Newcastle. That was pretty grim, wasn't it? Especially in winter. Well, that was a paradise of light and colour compared to Darkland. As for here—" He gestured to our lush surroundings. "I don't know where this is or even how I get here."

I was silent for a moment, trying to discover any meaning in my brother's words.

"You said that we won't be able to carry on meeting," I said, trying to make it not sound like an accusation.

"Not like we have been. This place and seeing you has something to do with why I haven't moved on, but I don't know how they are connected. At least, not yet. I think we *will* keep meeting for a little longer, but not just to chit-chat like two girls. There's something more important we have to talk about, or do."

"But what could it be?" Despite the bright sunlight on the back of my neck, the hairs that grew there stood to attention.

"Believe me, Johnny, if I knew I'd tell you. I have no idea what it could be at the moment, except that it involves—" He broke off and glanced away.

"Involves what, Cal? You have to tell me what you know. I'm not a kid any more."

He looked at me. "No," he said. "You're certainly not. All right. The only thing I'm certain about is that whatever I have to do involves protecting you.

"Little brother, you're in very grave danger."

Mary

If there is one thing that can be said with any degree of certainty about the British weather, it is this: it is entirely unpredictable.

British people have a reputation for talking about the weather. It is entirely justified. In lands where hot, dry summers and freezing, white winters are guaranteed, there's little to discuss. In Britain, there's nothing guaranteed about the weather other than there will be some. So people discuss it.

The summer of 1947 was a rarity. One of the few British summers that I have experienced that can truly be described as glorious. For a period of ten weeks or so, from early June, the sun shone brightly and constantly. The very occasional light shower did little more than dampen down the dust and provide some brief respite to parched flora.

What a time to be seventeen and in love.

As May ended, the last moisture was wrung from the sky and June arrived, bright and shiny as a new pin. Only a few wispy tendrils of cloud floated lazily across the wide blue sky like an afterthought. It was weather made for exploring.

Once or twice I accompanied Ma and Gwen on long afternoon walks in the surrounding countryside. They strolled leisurely, chatting and stopping frequently to exclaim over some wild flower or other. They were content to stick to major paths, ignoring the multitude of faintly defined paths that criss-crossed the main tracks and which looked a great deal more interesting to me.

With the onset of warm, dry days, I decided to explore on my own. I quickly developed a routine whereby my chores would be finished by mid morning, leaving the rest of the day to do with as I pleased. Gwen would prepare a simple picnic lunch and I'd set off, swinging the brown paper lunch bag jauntily by my side.

My favourite route was through the field behind Black Tops, past the lifeless pond—I invariably found myself increasing my pace until I was well clear of the murky water—and striking in a straight line for the ocean, around three miles away across gently sloping wood- and moorland.

The edge of the field was marked by a small wooded area, little more than a copse. No sooner would I enter the shaded canopy of trees than I noticed the sound of birdsong. This would inevitably set me off puzzling as to why they did not sing within the village, but I had no real idea so quickly stopped wondering. When you're seventeen and exploring a new, exciting environment, you don't get bogged down with conundrums that there's little hope of solving.

Once clear of the woods, the grass beneath my feet became coarser until it gave way to scrubland, thickly studded with gorse and heather. I followed narrow paths that I assumed had been made by rabbits and foxes, though could have been made by wolves or wild boar for all I knew.

If the breeze was blowing into my face, I would smell the ocean before I saw it. A sharp, tangy scent that I could almost taste and that set my pulse quickening. Then it would come into view over the dipping horizon, distant and mysterious, twinkling like sapphire in the sunlight.

As I drew nearer to the rocky coastline, the call of seabirds would reach me on the breeze. Although I did not know the different species at first (I subsequently learned their names in a book of Gwen's), all manner of birds circled and wheeled above the cliffs and sea. Cormorants, shags, terns, black-headed gulls and a host of other varieties of gull. Their noise filled the air as I approached the end of the land.

The first time that I reached the sea, I sank to the ground near the cliff edge and watched for an hour in rapt astonishment. I had never seen so many birds in one place. Of course, Newcastle had birds. Sparrows, thrushes, magpies and tits in the suburbs; pigeons underfoot in the city thoroughfares; gulls in abundance at the docks. Ugly, dirty, scrawny creatures those dockland gulls had been. Scabby, mustardy beaks and glaring, alien eyes. They were scavengers, fighting each other over scraps from the trawlers. Their calls harsh and bad-tempered, constantly yelling at one another as they squabbled over fish guts.

What a complete contrast these Cornish birds made. They leapt from nesting places in the cliffs and soared triumphantly through the clear air, gliding gracefully or playfully chasing each other. From their gullets came throaty chuckles of pleasure or mad whoops that sounded as though they were exulting in their unrestrained freedom and the wild splendour of their home.

The towering cliffs of the coastline had been formed from granite, thrust skywards in some prehistoric cataclysm. In places, seams of a softer, more crumbly rock intruded and had been eroded by the wind and rain. Surface water runoff had also taken advantage of the softer rock and the occasional stream chattered its way to the sea. It was fairly easy to clamber down the sloping sides of the resulting inlets and valleys to gain the beach below. I spent many a contented hour ambling aimlessly along the shingly shoreline, pausing now and then to throw a few pebbles at the waves or to examine an interesting lump of driftwood or stranded jellyfish.

On one occasion, I rather foolishly fell asleep on the beach. I ate my lunch resting against a large rock that was surprisingly comfortable. It was the day after one of my nocturnal visits to the Meadow and I felt dog tired. A full stomach, warm sun, rhythmic whoosh of breakers and joyful cries of birds all combined to lull me into slumber. I awoke to waves breaking over my outstretched legs. Luckily I had enough time to scamper back along the beach to where I could regain the moor without becoming any wetter. Had I fallen asleep closer to the foot of the cliff, I would have been in trouble. There would have been nobody around to hear my increasingly desperate cries for help as the water rose.

It was during one of my expeditions to the sea that I met Mary.

Wandering along the top of the cliffs late one afternoon, I came across one of the streams that had cut a path through softer rock and tinkled its way down to the beach. It looked as though the stream had come from roughly the direction of the village so I decided to follow its course as I headed homewards.

It made for a pleasantly diverting stroll. The cleft down which the water ran grew shallower as I walked inland, presumably as the bedrock became harder. The volume of water in the stream had not yet receded, despite the start of what would become a drought before the summer was out. It must have been fed by more than just rainwater. Maybe a spring—they weren't uncommon in the area.

The stream curved in gentle arcs as it sought the line of least resistance. In some places it was narrow, no more than three feet across. In others, it formed gently rippling pools, perhaps ten feet wide and three feet deep, into one of which I eagerly thrust my baking feet. Tiny silver fish darted up to my feet and away again like loosed arrows when I wiggled my toes at them.

The evening sun was still strong enough to dry my feet. Grudgingly, I thrust them back into the battered heavy workshoes that I always wore and continued upstream.

As I drew nearer to the village, the stream meandered into a wooded area. The trees, many old and gnarled, either stood apart or grew together in small knots like groups of gossiping pensioners. Wide avenues ran through the wood and I passed through glades that the sun dappled in orange-tinted shadows.

When I first heard the sound, I thought it must be some new type of birdsong that I hadn't heard before. I was not yet so close to Tregeagle that the birds had grown mute.

As I drew closer to the sound's source, I realised that this was no bird. It was someone humming a tune. Whoever it was, they were hidden from view by a clump of trees that grew thickly together along the bank of the stream.

I proceeded cautiously, making as little noise as possible. Studiously avoiding fallen twigs and protruding leafy branches, I made my way past the knot of trees. Any noise I did make must have been muffled by the chattering of the brook for the humming didn't falter.

The trees petered out into a wide, sunlit clearing. The ground grew thickly with verdant grass that reminded me of the Meadow. Lying in the grass, eyes closed, humming, was a girl.

I stood and stared. Her head was turned away from me towards the sinking sun. She had long dark hair that pooled around her head like spilled molasses. She wore a cotton short-sleeved shirt that revealed darkly tanned arms. Her skirt looked coarse. It was pulled up to her bent knees. As I gazed upon her brown, muscular calves, she opened and shut her legs as though to waft cooling air into her skirt and I caught a glimpse of inner thigh. Smooth and milky. I swallowed hard.

Clearing my throat wasn't easy my mouth had become bone dry but I managed some sort of noise and walked forward as though I had only just appeared from around the bend.

The humming immediately stopped and her head jerked in my direction. The last of the day's sunlight made her hair glow like burnished ebony.

Seeing me approach, the girl scrambled to her feet. In the brief confusion of whirling skirt, I was treated to another glimpse of thigh. My breath caught in my chest and I stopped walking, not wanting to frighten her away.

"H-h-hello," I managed. Through the pounding in my ears, my voice sounded thin and reedy.

The girl looked to be about eighteen and was exceptionally pretty. She considered me warily from large, dark eyes. She seemed poised to take to her heels like a startled doe.

I attempted a smile as I studied her more closely. She stood a few inches shorter than me but was nevertheless unusually tall for a girl in those days. She was slim, though not skinny. As far as I could tell, she curved handsomely in all the right places. Her face was also tanned a deep brown, lending an impression that she came from Romanic stock, though she wore no bangles, ear-rings or other adornments that may have reinforced that impression.

The girl's lips were full and began to turn up at the corners as I realised that I was gawping once more. Her hands moved to her hips and she relaxed her stance. One eyebrow rose enquiringly. I attempted speech again.

"I'm s-sorry if I startled you. I was just following the steam back to the village—no, I mean *stream*, though in this heat it could easily turn into steam. The stream, that is. . . ." My mind was galloping and my mouth could not keep up.

As I tailed off like some sun-baked half-wit, the girl giggled. In my heightened state of anxiety, it sounded more like a throaty chuckle that made my blood pound harder. She stepped forward and held out her hand. I took it in mine, expecting to be grasping a wad of silk. Instead, my grip was returned firmly. Her hand felt tough and callused. As we shook, I gazed into eyes that were big and wide and brown. Pools of molten ebony that I would gladly have drowned in.

"My name's Mary," she said. "You're Miss Evans's nephew." Her accent was rich and rolling and undulating. She sounded like the man I had met in the village pub, though there the resemblance ended. While his face had been slack and vacuous, Mary's was bursting with life and intelligence and humour.

"Aye, that I be." I immediately regretted my clumsy mockery of her accent.

But instead of taking offence, she made a fair attempt at mimicking my northern brogue. "Howay, man. You're from Newcastle, why aye?"

We looked at each other and burst into laughter. It felt good to laugh and my tension evaporated.

"My name's John," I said. "Do you live in Tregeagle?"

"Where else? There's no other village within ten miles of here. I've seen you fetching water from the pump. I live on the other side of the green from you."

"Why didn't you come out and say hello?" I felt a little peeved. I had been starting to think that the other villagers must have been suffering from some rare disease that kept them indoors. All the time this gorgeous creature had been hiding away in one of the cottages.

Mary shook her head. "Da don't like me mixing with other villagers. Besides, I knew we'd be bound to bump into each other away from prying eyes." Her eyebrows rose fractionally and I felt my breath hitch in my chest again. This girl could stop me in my tracks with the simplest of gestures.

"I was on my way back to the village. Would you like to walk with me?"

"No. But thanks for asking. I'll be heading for home soon enough, but I'm not ready yet."

I was reluctant to take my leave of her. "Will you be all right on your own?"

She snorted. "I've been coming out to these woods on me own all my life. Are you sure *you* will be all right on *your* own?"

"Yeah, stupid question." I smiled ruefully then nodded upstream. "Can I follow the stream all the way to the village?"

"More or less. When it bends sharply to the left, leave it and follow the path to the right. That'll take you back to the village."

"Thanks. I'll be off then." I made no effort to move.

Her lips curved into the knowing smile that I would become so familiar with. "I'll see you soon, John."

"Great! But how . . . ?"

"Oh, I'm out this way most afternoons. We'll bump into each other again."

"Away from prying eyes?" My boldness surprised me.

Her smile grew broader and, if this was possible, sexier.

I smiled too, turned away and walked home, whistling all the way.

The Glade

It is said that beauty is in the eye of the beholder and I guess that is one of the truer sayings. Perhaps other men would not have considered Mary to have been as ravishingly beautiful as I did, difficult though I find that to believe. She made the girls I'd fooled around with in Newcastle seem frumpish by comparison. It is true that I encountered women throughout the ensuing sixty years whose earthy sexuality at least matched Mary's, but none who surpassed it.

Never have I met someone who has made such a profound impression upon me in such a brief space of time. The night after that first encounter, I went to sleep thinking about her. I awoke thinking about her. I dreamed about her. Ordinary dreams, not like the ones in which I met Callum, and often steamingly erotic, though not seedy. Tender.

I didn't see her again for almost a week after that initial meeting. I returned to the glade next to the stream each afternoon. I went there so regularly that I came to think of it as the Glade. I'd arrive at a forced saunter, trying to give every appearance of just happening to be passing that way, while my stomach churned in anticipation of seeing her once more. When she wasn't there I'd collapse deflated into the long grass and wait in case she came by.

There were less picturesque places to pass time. The grassy area sloped gently upwards from the stream at an angle ideal for lying and appreciating the scenery. The grass was lush and soft despite the lack of rain, probably nourished by groundwater from the stream, and made a comfortable resting place. Water babbled along the rocky bed of the stream, forming tiny spectrums of colour in the sunlight where the surface was churned into miniature rapids by protruding pebbles or roots. Occasionally, a multi-hued dragonfly darted across the surface, wings a blur. Sometimes small birds chased the dragonflies, or each other, skimming the water and chirruping like excited children. Grasshoppers added their music to the countryside symphony.

The woods grew thicker on the other side of the stream in a profusion of shades of green, too many to count. Rays of sunlight speared the gaps between the trees, spotlighting motes of dust or seedlings in a lazy dance like plankton floating through an ocean.

On this side of the stream, trees formed a rough semi-circle at the top of the slope, giving the comforting impression of concealment and privacy.

I spent hours lying in the grass. When the sun became uncomfortably hot, I'd lie at the foot of the slope with my feet in the water, or at the head of the slope in the shade of the trees. Occasionally I'd snooze. Usually I'd contemplate.

It's funny what things go through our minds when we are relaxed and have little to do but think. I was seventeen and my thoughts were unburdened by profound, philosophical issues like the meaning of life. I daydreamed about scoring the winning goal for Newcastle United in the FA Cup Final at Wembley or becoming a Hollywood film star or, and most often, sex. Sometimes I wondered about such great imponderables as why women needed razorblades, why all babies were ugly and quite what exactly were chilblains. That last one worried me a little. I had heard talk of catching chilblains in winter and they sounded something to be avoided.

Of course, I also spent a great deal of time thinking about Mary.

One morning at the breakfast table, I asked Gwen about Mary. I tried to keep my tone casual.

"Auntie Gwen, do you know a girl in the village called Mary?"

I didn't miss Gwen's quick glance at Ma and the sudden twinkle in her eyes. Despite my determination to present a cool exterior, I could already feel the first flush forming at the base of my neck.

"Hmm," said Gwen. "Hmm . . . Mary, you say? Let me think."

I was aware that Ma had placed her cutlery down, though she hadn't finished her breakfast, and was watching me closely. I couldn't look at her. The warmth was spreading up the back of my head and down my shoulderblades.

"Um, Mary, Mary. . . ." said Gwen. "Dark hair? About your age?"

I nodded.

"Yes," said Gwen. "Of course. You must mean Mary Fletcher. Lives with her father the other side of the green. Took me a moment to recall her as you hardly ever see her about."

"Hardly ever see anybody about in this village," said Ma.

Gwen nodded. "People do keep to themselves around here. That's why I like it. Hmm . . . Mary Fletcher. Why do you want to know about her, Johnny Boy?"

I groaned silently. Gwen only called me Johnny Boy when she was in teasing mode.

Feigning complete indifference, I replied airily, "Oh, I happened to bump into her when I was out walking the other day."

Gwen glanced at Ma and then back at me, an innocent expression on her face. "Pretty girl, that Mary. Very pretty indeed. Wouldn't you agree, Johnny Boy?"

"Mm." I tried my best to make the grunt sound non-committal and bent my head to examine the remains of my breakfast.

It was too quiet. I glanced back up, as they knew I would, to find Gwen and Ma staring intently at me, huge, foolish grins lighting up their faces. Instantly, the flush enveloped my head.

"Bit hot in here this morning, love," remarked Ma. Their grins spread even wider.

"Running a touch of fever, Johnny Boy?" said Gwen.

Mustering as much dignity as is possible with brightly blazing cheeks, I rose to my feet and strode out to the garden. I could hear them dissolve into gleeful giggles as I pulled the door closed behind me.

The day after Callum warned me that I was in danger, I went to the Glade as usual in the afternoon. For the first time, my primary motive in going there wasn't the hope of seeing Mary. After five or six fruitless visits to the Glade, I had started to give up hope of bumping into her again.

On this day, my thoughts were troubled at my brother's words and I wanted to be somewhere quiet where I might ponder them. And as usual following one of my night-time liaisons with Callum, I was worn out.

I arrived at the Glade about an hour or so after noon. It was a breathless day; I could almost see the sun bleaching the colour from the grass in the fields that I passed through on my way. I flopped thankfully into the shade of the trees and closed my eyes.

The atmosphere had subtly changed in that dream world I called the Meadow. Callum's mood had changed. I did not think that we would be spending any more time together there—if 'time' is the correct word—taking nostalgic trips to our childhoods in Newcastle. Whatever the purpose of the meetings might be, it appeared to be something more than merely allowing me to see my brother again. I would have to rely on Callum learning more in that place between worlds he called Darkland.

At least I had stopped doubting my sanity and come to accept the Meadow, if not as reality then as *a* reality. I wasted no more time in wondering how such a place might exist. There was still enough child in me to acknowledge that some things were beyond my ability to understand.

Similarly, the childlike part prevented me from worrying excessively about Callum's warning. He didn't know what form the danger took or where I might encounter it. Until he could be more specific, there was nothing to be gained by fretting. Children are accustomed to adults warning them of unseen dangers. Of sinister highways with murderous motorists; of mysterious strangers with sugary smiles and treats; of lakes with grasping weeds. As children, we file these warnings away to be retrieved if required but to sit quietly, gathering mental dust, if not.

And that is what I did with Callum's warning. I examined it, shook it, prodded it and then filed it away. In so doing, my tension evaporated and I slipped peacefully into slumber.

I had grown adept at estimating the passage of time from the position of the sun, which was rarely hidden by cloud that summer. When I awoke in the Glade, I could make out the sun through the mesh of leaves and guessed that I had slept for about two hours. Despite being in the shade, I felt hot and sticky.

Then an angel blocked my view. A dusky, sensual angel. It was leaning over, peering into my sleepy face. It held a stalk of grass in one hand that it brushed against my nose.

"Hey, that tickles," I said, sitting up to stretch.

"You're lucky," said Mary. "I did think about putting woodlice in your mouth as you snored."

"I do not snore," I protested. " . . . do I?"

"It sounded like someone sawing wood." She laughed lightly and sat next to me on the grass. Her hair was tied back into a ponytail that served to emphasise her graceful jawline and prominent cheekbones. She wore a simple but pretty dress that tautened seductively at hip and bosom. How I yearned to run my fingers along those fine lines.

"You all right?" I asked.

"Yes . . . why?" She looked puzzled.

"Um, I meant, how are you?" Some of that tongue-tied awkwardness that had hampered me during our first meeting was creeping back. I willed it away.

"Oh, I'm fine, thanks," said Mary. "And you?"

"I'm fine too." I grunted. "We're being very polite and proper, aren't we? I mean, I'm really glad that we've bumped into each other again. I don't want to just sit and make small talk."

"What *do* you want to do?" She gazed at me intently as if daring me to speak my mind.

I could feel myself starting to blush. If Mary was inviting me to be candid, I didn't have the courage to accept.

"What I mean," I said, "is that I'd like to get to know you. I've hardly met anyone else who lives around here and the ones I have met, well. . . ."

"Bit strange, aren't they," she said, "the other people in the village."

"I'm glad *you* said that. Why does nobody ever seem to step outside their front door? I've been here almost two months and I've barely seen another person. It's weird."

Mary shrugged. "I've noticed it too. I've lived here all my life and it can get very lonely."

"Haven't you ever had the urge to get away?"

"Every day I dream about escaping from Tregeagle. There are so many places I'd like to visit." A wistful, faraway look appeared briefly in her face, then was gone. "But I've no money, no trade. Furthest I've ever been is to the market in town."

"What about school? There isn't one in the village. You must have gone to one away from here?"

She shook her head. "Never been to school in my life."

"But how—?" I broke off, uncertain.

"How what?"

"You speak so well. As if you've been educated."

"Not like a country bumpkin, you mean?"

"Yes. I mean, no." I shrugged. "Oh, pay no attention to me. I'm just a city boy from up north. What do I know?"

Mary laid a hand on my forearm. My skin tingled at her touch. I sat very still.

"I said that I'd never attended school," she said, "not that I've never had an education. After my mother died, my dad's sister came to live with us. She was much older than him. She used to be a teacher."

"So she taught you."

"I probably learned to read sooner than most children. My aunt was very patient. She taught me to love books and now I can never get enough to read." She took her hand from my arm and drew up her knees, clasping her arms around them. "My mother died when I was a baby. I never knew her. I suppose my aunt became my mother-figure, though she would have hated me saying that. She died when I was twelve. I still miss her." She sighed and I felt an urge to put my arm around her shoulders. But I couldn't; not yet.

"My Aunt Gwen and me Ma always have their noses in books," I said. "I could ask if you can borrow some."

Mary smiled. "Yes, I'd like that. Even if I never get to see the world, I love reading about it."

"You could travel . . . see the world. If you had someone to go with you." I still lacked the courage to add *Me, for instance* but she knew what I was getting at.

"You're sweet," she said, "but I can't leave. He needs me."

"*He*? Oh." My heart sank.

"My father." My heart resurfaced. "I sometimes think that he hates me and I sometimes hate him back. But he'd be lost without me."

"Why do you think he hates you? Oh sorry, that's none of my business."

"It's okay. I don't mind telling you. I feel that I can trust you."

"You can. I feel the same way about you." It was true. I hardly knew this girl yet she felt like an old and trusted friend.

Mary sighed heavily. "My mother died giving birth to me. My parents were quite old to be starting a family and there were complications. My father blames me for my mother's death. He blames me for denying him a son. Sometimes he makes me wish I'd never been born." A single tear rolled down her cheek, leaving a damp streak. I longed to wipe it away, to take her in my arms and comfort her. But still I dared not.

"But," she said, sitting straighter, "he's still my father. It's my duty to stay with him and look after him. To help with the garden and the animals."

I understood. I felt a similar sense of duty towards Ma, though mine was in no way onerous.

"Well," I said, "one day you'll be free to follow your own path. What will you do then? In the future?"

She didn't answer immediately. Her expression did not lighten. If anything, it grew darker.

"You don't understand," she said. "I have no future." With that, she rose to her feet.

She was right, I didn't understand. "Don't go. I'm sorry if I upset you."

She looked down at me and forced a smile. She looked beautiful, tearstains and all. "You didn't upset me, John. I have to go now but I'll be back this way tomorrow afternoon."

"I'll see you then?"

"You might." Now her smile looked more natural.

She turned and headed back towards the village. My gaze followed her until she was lost from sight in the trees.

That evening, buoyed from my afternoon nap and unexpected encounter with Mary, I was still wide awake when Ma and Gwen turned in for the night. I decided to remain in the kitchen and read for a while by the light of the huge oil lamp that hung above the table and cast a much brighter light than the small lamp that I carried up to my bedroom each night.

Although I had not yet acquired my mother's and aunt's love of reading—that wasn't to come until late into my twenties—there was little else to do in the evenings. So I pulled a book at random from Gwen's collection of classics and settled down to read. It was Swift's weird and wonderful adventures of Gulliver. At first, I struggled with the archaic style of writing, but soon found myself embroiled in Gulliver's strange sojourns. By the time sleepiness found me, Gulliver was in the clutches of the diminutive Lilliputians—at the mercy of midgets, it could be said.

I lit my small lamp before extinguishing the kitchen lamp. Immediately the shadows drew in, jostling like queuing children. I made my way up the creaking stairs.

Four rooms led off the landing: three bedrooms and a box room that Gwen used for storage. My bedroom was at the back of the house, next to the box room. Ma and Gwen slept in the bedrooms at the front of the house.

The doors to each room were of a dark, heavy wood. When all four were closed, as now, the landing was cast in inky blackness. I was glad of the meagre, flickering light cast by the lamp I carried.

I was heading for my bedroom when I heard a noise. I stood stock-still and strained my ears to catch it again.

There. It was coming from Gwen's room.

I moved quietly to stand outside her bedroom door. The door was thick and muffled sounds from within. It sounded like a voice, a woman's voice. I could not tell what it was saying. I pressed my ear tight to the door. Now I could hear more clearly, although it was still difficult to make out complete sentences, only the odd word or phrase. Gwen seemed to be holding a conversation, presumably in her sleep. I caught the word 'forgiveness' and the phrase 'he seduced me'. I guessed that she was dreaming about her youth and the incident that resulted in her being exiled from her village in shame.

I was just about to turn away when I heard something that made my blood run cold. It was a man's voice. Deep and guttural, almost a growl. It was much louder than Gwen's and I could hear every word.

"Harlot! Whore of Babylon! You wanted him to fuck you. You begged him to, you bitch!"

I didn't pause to wonder who the speaker might be or how he had gained entrance to the house. I twisted the brass doorknob with my free hand and burst into the room. I raised the lamp above my head in the hope of dazzling the intruder.

Gwen was crouched into a foetal position at the head of the bed. The bedclothes were thrust towards the foot of the bed as though kicked there. Gwen faced towards me. Her eyes were tightly shut and she whimpered softly. She was fast asleep.

She was also alone.

Dead Lights

After making sure that there were no intruders hiding under the bed or in the wardrobe, I drew the bedcovers over my aunt, who had stopped whimpering and settled into a more peaceful sleep, and went across the landing to my bedroom.

I lay in bed puzzling over what had happened. The only rational explanation I could come up with was that my aunt had spoken in a man's voice while in the grip of her nightmare. My entrance must have broken the nightmare without waking her.

There were irrational explanations too but I tried to push them from my mind, telling myself that it was possible for a person under extreme stress, as Gwen had been in the throes of the nightmare, to speak in a voice wholly unlike their own.

But I wasn't convinced and sleep eluded me.

My bedroom had two small windows that overlooked the back garden and the field beyond. With the onset of fine weather, I had taken to leaving the heavy drapes undrawn and the windows open as wide as they would go to take advantage of any night-time breezes. The ancient double bed in which I slept occupied the opposite wall. It was a wonderful start to a new day to awake to the sun's rays slanting through the windows and the scent of honeysuckle borne on the breeze. I didn't even mind the occasional waft of pig ordure, once I had grown accustomed to it.

That night I tossed and turned. The full moon had departed from the sky a week or more previously. It was still hours before dawn and it was therefore disconcerting to become aware of the bedroom gradually becoming lighter. At first I put it down to my sleepless eyes becoming more accustomed to the darkness, giving the illusion that it was actually becoming brighter. Or that my imagination, buoyed by the earlier fright, was over-active. But, no: the room was becoming appreciably lighter with every passing minute.

I swung my legs off the bed and padded to the nearest window. I peered out.

The moon was not in sight. There were stars aplenty, their pale luminosity partially obscured by lazy wisps of cloud. They were not the cause of my bedroom becoming lighter. The source seemed to be much closer to home.

It took me a few moments to pinpoint the precise location. The field behind the rear garden of Black tops was glowing in a cold, blue-tinged light. The glow was spilling into the garden. I could see Bangers and Mash pacing in their pen, disorientated by the unnatural brightness at an hour when it should have been dark.

The light was emanating from about the position where the pond lay, the one from which I'd tried in vain to catch newts or tadpoles. It took me a moment or two more to realise that the pond *was* the source of the light.

Even as I watched, the intensity of the light began to lessen. Had I ever seen a dimmer switch at that point in my life, that's what it would have reminded me of: someone turning off an electric light very slowly but steadily using a dimmer switch.

The pigs grunted softly as the light faded from the garden. Shadowy darkness crept along the path of the diminishing glow. A minute or so later, the light had disappeared altogether and nighttime resumed.

I remained at the window for a while, watching to see if the glow would return. With no further sign of it and with the burn of sleepiness at last making itself felt behind my eyelids, I returned to bed.

My last thoughts before I sank into slumber were of the cold blue light. I had heard of phosphorescence, the phenomenon where tiny aquatic animals glow in the dark. The starlight and any other relevant factors must have been at precisely the right level to trigger off a brief display of phosphorescence. So I thought.

The fact that the pond was singularly devoid of any sort of life, let alone exotic phosphorescent creatures, did not occur to me.

The following morning at the breakfast table, I watched Gwen closely. If she was suffering any after effect of her night terrors, she didn't show it.

As we sat drinking our cups of tea in companionable silence, I cleared my throat.

"I noticed a strange light behind the house last night. A bluish light. It was coming from that old pond."

"Hmm?" said Ma. "What sort of light, love?"

"Not really sure. More a glow than anything else."

"From the pond you say?" said Gwen.

I nodded. "It lit up the field and my bedroom. That's how I noticed it."

"You hadn't been at the wine again, Johnny Boy?" Gwen's eyes sparkled with mischief.

"Nope. And I wasn't dreaming either. I was wide awake and sober."

"Then it must have been the Dead Lights of Tregeagle." I glanced at her, catching the surreptitious wink she made to Ma.

"What are dead lights, Auntie Gwen?" I asked innocently.

"Oh, every now and again the souls of all the people who have ever lived and died in Tregeagle gather together in one place."

I leaned forward, opening my eyes wide. "*Really?*"

"Aye." Gwen nodded sagely, also leaning forward, warming to her theme. "When all them poor wandering souls meet, their melded energy produces a blue ghostly aura."

"Melted energy?" I was enjoying myself.

"Not melted, *twp*." Gwen rolled her eyes. "Didn't they teach you anything in school? *Melded*, you know, joined together."

"Ah," I said. "So why do they all get together, these ghosts?"

"It's said. . . ." Gwen leaned further forward so that her ample bosom pressed against the edge of the table and her voice dropped to a stage whisper. "It's said that they come back to take revenge on those who wronged them when they were alive. They roam into the night seeking out those wrongdoers, and when they find them. . . ."

"Yes?" I breathed.

"The wrongdoers are doomed."

"What happens to them?"

"It's simple, but terrible. The ghosts steal their souls."

I breathed out heavily. "That's it? If you're going to make up a story, it should have a better ending than that. I know you were making that up. I saw you wink at Ma."

Ma laughed. "No flies on my boy, Gwen." She stood and started to clear away the breakfast dishes.

Gwen leaned back, a wry smile on her face. The mischievous twinkle had disappeared from her eyes. "Fair enough. I was making it up. Most of it anyway. . . ."

I narrowed my eyes. "What d'you mean, most of it?"

Gwen pursed her lips as though debating whether to go on. Then she leaned forward again and rested her arms on the kitchen table.

"Well," she said. "I don't know what that blue light really is, but it's not the first time I've heard about it."

"Really?" This time I wasn't feigning interest.

"I fetched up in this village, what... let's see, about twenty or so years ago. Something had happened to one of the villagers a few years before. Something not very nice. On the green in full view of everyone. People were still talking about it years later."

"What, people talked to each other? *Here?*"

Gwen arched her eyebrows. "You've noticed that, have you? Yeah, everyone keeps themselves to themselves now. But it hasn't always been like that."

Ma rejoined us at the table. "I've noticed it too," she said. "Can hardly miss it. Very unfriendly lot around here."

Gwen nodded.

"So what happened?" I asked, impatient to hear more about the light.

Gwen glanced at Ma. "You sure you want to hear this? It's not a pleasant tale."

Ma looked at me and I nodded fervently. Ma shrugged.

"Okay," said Gwen. "I'd only been in Tregeagle for a few months, but I had become friendly with the innkeeper's wife. She died about ten years ago during the flu outbreak. You've met her son."

I thought back to our arrival in Tregeagle and nodded. "He directed us to Black Tops. He's a little, er, dim."

"That's putting it politely," said Gwen. "Anyway, she told me about Jez Kellock. As far as I can recall her words, this is what she said. . . ."

"Jez Kellock lived in a two-room cottage the other side of the village. A bitter and twisted man he was. Nobody liked him. Rumour had it that he'd killed his wife. Smothered her as she slept with a feather pillow. Couldn't be proved though. The constabulary came from town and poked around but no charges were ever laid against Jez. Still, people talked.

"One day, Jez disappeared. People said they'd seen a blue, glowing light during the night that surrounded Jez Kellock's cottage like a mist. One or two said they'd heard screams. In the morning, villagers forced their way into his cottage, fearing to find the man murdered. But there was no sign of him.

"For days later, people living the other side of the village claimed they heard noises in the forest behind their houses. Shouts, screams, breaking branches. A group of men ventured into the forest, but found nothing.

"Then, about five days after he'd disappeared, Jez Kellock came back. He stumbled into the village green. No-one saw where he came from, but one or two people noticed him on the green. Their shouts and screams brought the rest of the village out to see what was going on. It was a terrible sight.

"Jez Kellock had jet black hair. It had started to grey at the temples, and thin a little, but was still as dark as an Italian's. The hair on the man standing on the village green was white. White as snow, and wispy, as if Jez had aged thirty years in less than a week. He twitched and jumped as though demons danced inside him. And his eyes . . . his gaze was wild and uncomprehending and darted from side to side, seeing things that we could not. His clothes were little more than rags. He was gibbering, spit dribbling from his lips, speaking words we couldn't understand.

"No-one approached him, not even the men. We were too afraid.

"Jez had something clutched in one fist. A short stick, each end sharpened to a point. The wood was stained dark. From the cuts and blood that covered his arms, his thighs, his chest, it looked as though he had been gouging himself with the stick in his derangement. As we watched, he dropped to his knees and thrust one end of the stick into the ground. The earth was soft from rain and the stick went in easily. Leaning forward, he grasped the stick with both hands where it protruded from the ground.

"We could tell what he intended to do. Someone moaned, 'No, no, don't . . .' But nobody made a move to stop him.

"Jez Kellock knelt on the grass and stared at the stick. The point was about a foot from his face. He looked as though he were in chapel praying with his hands clasped before him like that. Then he lifted his head and looked at us. For the first time he seemed to see us. He shouted out, his only coherent words: 'Ware the Dead Lights!' Once more: 'Ware the Dead Lights!' He voice was loud but empty, as though he was already dead.

"He turned his attention back to the stick that he still gripped tightly in both hands. Nobody moved. Nobody turned away, though many of us wanted to. Jez uttered one final shriek. A shrill, forlorn, hopeless sound. Then, in one sudden movement, he rammed his face down onto the end of the stick.

"His aim was good. The stick punched through his right eye and into his brain. Men cried out. Women screamed. Children—yes, there were children watching too—at last looked away and buried their faces in their mothers' aprons.

"Jez's grip on the stick had loosened in the moment of death. His arms dangled to the ground. He had slumped forward on his knees, the stick strong enough to support his head. Rivulets of blood ran down it and soaked into the ground.

"By the time anyone plucked up enough courage to step forward and cover the body, the grass around the stick had turned a wide circle of bright red."

"Oh my God, Gwen, that's a bloody horrible story!" Ma looked quite pale.

Gwen shook herself and blew heavily through her mouth. "Aye," she said. "Perhaps I should have left out the gory bits, but that's how it was told to me. Sorry, *cariad*, I got a bit carried away there."

"You bloody well ought to be carried away sometimes. Honestly, Gwen." With that, Ma rose to her feet and strode outside to the lavatory to perform her morning ablutions.

"Auntie Gwen," I said after the back door had closed behind Ma. "Do you believe that story?"

"Not really. Mind you, the innkeeper's wife believed it. I could see it in her eyes." She shrugged. "But just because someone believes something's true, doesn't make it so. And yet. . . ."

"And yet?" I prompted.

"Well, when I was telling that story, although I didn't believe it had really happened, it's almost as if. . . ."

"Almost as if it's something that *could* have happened here?"

"Ye-es, I think that's it. Or something that *should* have happened here."

"Perhaps it did happen. It would help explain why people hide themselves away."

"It hasn't always been like this, you know, love. People in Tregeagle were quite reserved when I first got here, but I got to know a lot of them just from fetching water. And the tavern was then the hub of the village. But gradually it tailed off. People started staying indoors. By the time she died, I hadn't spoken to the innkeeper's wife for two years. And we used to be friends. I don't know how the tavern remains open. Or why."

"Hmm," I muttered. "This is a very strange place. Auntie Gwen, have you ever noticed that the birds don't sing within the village?"

She laughed. Then she frowned. "Are you serious, *cariad?* That's a bit too strange, even for Tregeagle."

"It's true though. Go anywhere in the village, even your back garden, and you won't hear the call of a bird. Walk two hundred yards away in any direction and the air will be full of their cries."

"Come to think of it," said Gwen, nodding her head slowly, "I rarely notice birds in the garden. Used to leave food out in the winter, but it was hardly ever taken. Don't do it any more. It all goes to the pigs. Most peculiar."

"Another thing that's peculiar is that blue light. You said it appeared around that man's cottage, that Jez bloke, before he killed himself."

"That's just a story, love. Don't pay it any heed."

"But I saw it for myself. Last night. It's real. Maybe that part of the story is true. And maybe what you said earlier is true, about it being all the lost souls of the village coming together."

Gwen sat straighter. "Now that part was definitely made up. By me."

My shoulders sagged. "Pity. Would have made a good name: The Village of Lost Souls."

We lapsed into a few moments of silence, each of us busy with our own thoughts. Ma was still outside. The tale of Jez Kellock must have upset her. I was just considering going to check if she was all right when it occurred to me that now would be a good time to raise the earlier incident from last night, while Gwen was in a relatively garrulous mood.

"Auntie Gwen?"

"Yes, love?"

"You were having a bad dream when I came upstairs to go to bed last night."

"Oh, that's nothing unusual. Talking in my sleep was I?"

"Yeah, but . . . but I thought I heard a man. He was calling you horrible names. It sounded nothing like your voice. I came into your room, to try to protect you. But there was nobody else there."

Gwen leaned forward and laid a warm hand against my cheek. "Tried to protect me, *cariad*... thank you." Then her expression hardened and she withdrew her hand. She looked at me intently. "Haven't I told you before? It was my father. Or, at least, his ghost. A mean and spiteful ghost he is too."

I must have looked disbelieving.

"It's true, love, far-fetched as it sounds. You heard him speak. Like you said, his voice is nothing like mine."

I didn't say that I'd concluded the man's voice must have come from her own throat. I didn't know quite what to say. The things my aunt was telling me were crazy, impossible, yet she appeared perfectly sane. And I was already becoming accustomed to believing that things I'd hitherto thought impossible might be anything but. Holding conversations with a dead brother, for one.

"But why, Auntie Gwen? Why would your father's ghost say such horrible things to you?"

"Because I betrayed the family. Worse, I went against every good thing I'd ever been taught the day I desecrated his grave. I—" She broke off and glanced at the door. We could hear Ma approaching. "Shush now. Not a word of this to your mother. Besides thinking I'm nuts, it would break her heart."

That day turned out to be another scorcher. I left the village, chores completed, a little after noon. Despite my unsettling conversation with Gwen, there was a spring in my step at the thought of seeing Mary.

Once at the Glade, I cooled my feet in the brook before settling down in the shade to eat my picnic lunch. Barely had I started when Mary strolled into view, hands thrust casually into the patch pockets of the flowered summer dress that she wore. The sight of her once more took my breath away.

She smiled and sat down beside me. I motioned for her to join in my lunch. We ate chunks of bread and cheese, strips of cured pork, washed down with well water that was rapidly becoming tepid.

When we had finished, Mary lay back contentedly. She laced her hands behind her head, making her dress tighten across her breasts. I tried not to notice. She looked up at me.

"I was thinking," she said, "about what we spoke about yesterday. About Tregeagle being a strange place."

For a moment I wondered whether to tell her about my conversation with Gwen, but decided not to. For now.

"And?" I said.

"Well, I asked my father about it. He was in a good mood this morning. Makes a change. Anyway, he wouldn't say much but he as good as acknowledged that there's something odd about the place. He hinted that it has to do with something that happened here, a long time ago. When I started to press him for more, his mood darkened and I dared not go any further."

I wondered what sort of man could make his daughter so afraid of him. "Did he give any clues as to what happened?"

Mary shook her head. The action made her breasts shift slightly beneath the dress. I hurriedly turned my attention elsewhere.

"Enough of my father. Tell me about yourself, John."

"What's to tell?"

"Tell me about Newcastle. About your family. About your life before coming here."

"I'll bore you silly."

"I'd love to hear about it. Besides, I've already told you about myself. It's your turn." Her lip turned down in a mock pout. I laughed.

"All right, but don't say I didn't warn you."

So I talked. I told her about my childhood in Newcastle. I talked of my family. I related Callum's fight with Mitch Mahoney. I talked of Morfydd winning a prize for writing a short story. Of my father's quiet stolidity. Of my mother's refusal to bow to hardship.

Mary listened attentively, like a star pupil, interrupting occasionally with a question. Her eyes shone when I described the city and what life had been like there.

"Tell you what," I said impulsively. "Why don't I take you to Newcastle one day?"

"Yes," she said. "That would be lovely." But she didn't sound enthusiastic, as though part of her knew it would never happen.

When she urged me to continue, I told her about our lives during the war and our deaths. It was the first time I had spoken to anybody except Ma and Gwen about the losses of my brother and sister and, after the war, my father. She seemed to understand that it was painful and coaxed me gently through it.

I told her everything. Callum's leaving party. The St Christopher medallion I'd bought for him. The telegram. The visit from Private Black and the tale he had to tell. Morfydd's end during the Blitz. Da's descent into lingering decay and degradation. Along with this outpouring came a host of pent-up emotions I hadn't even realised I kept locked up inside. Anger, bitterness, frustration, despair, horror. Expelling them was like lancing a festering boil.

By the time I had finished talking, tears ran freely down my cheeks and I felt utterly drained. Mary took me tenderly in her arms and held me as she would a child. I buried my face into her luxurious hair and breathed her in. It was like breathing in pure oxygen. It made me lightheaded, giddy, but also revived me, banishing my exhaustion so that I felt capable of climbing a mountain. In that instant, I knew that I loved her.

At last, with great reluctance, I pulled out of her embrace. The sun was starting to sink below the trees on the opposite bank of the stream. I had talked the entire afternoon away.

I looked into Mary's eyes. "Thank you," I said.

"For what?"

"For listening. I hadn't realised how much I needed to get those things off my chest. I feel so much better now. Lighter somehow."

She smiled and I almost kissed her. But something still held me back.

"You and your mother have been through a lot," she said. "I'm not surprised she needed to get away." She dropped her gaze coyly. "I'm glad you came here to Tregeagle."

"So am I. Oh boy, so am I."

We linked arms companionably as we walked back to the village. I felt light-headed, almost gliding instead of walking. So this was love. It felt wonderful.

We parted as we reached the village. She leaned forward and placed a soft kiss on my cheek. As she pulled back she smiled, a smile that held the promise of so much more. I watched her head across the village green until she disappeared into her small cottage.

I turned and floated gently home.

A Frosty Reunion

It happened like all the other times: one moment asleep, the next full alertness. I was back in the Meadow. But this time there was something wrong.

As usual, I had come to lying on my stomach on the grass. Unlike the previous occasions, it was cold. Freezing cold.

The blades of grass resembled spun sugar and crunched beneath me as I scrambled to my feet. My breath billowed out in plumes like a car exhaust.

It was daylight, but gloomy as though it was late afternoon in winter. The light had the same sort of ethereal quality that can herald the coming of a thunderstorm. But there would be no thunder; it was too damn cold.

The field stretched away as far as I could see in every direction, like it always did, but instead of swathes of luxuriant grass rippling in the breeze, it looked as though the grass had been liberally doused with icing sugar and starched into stillness.

I stood uncertainly, hopping from foot to foot in a vain attempt to keep warm, and waited. A ball of apprehension appeared in my stomach, and grew.

At once I became aware that there was someone behind me. I turned.

In front of me stood a man in his early to mid twenties. I hadn't set eyes on him for about ten years and he'd been a teenager then. I would not have thought it possible, but he had filled out even more in manhood. He stood a few inches shorter than me but was still built like a brick shithouse, an even sturdier model. He was regarding me from eyes that had sunk into the surrounding flesh. Piggy eyes.

"Fuck me," he said. "If it isn't Baby Andrews."

"Hello, Mitch," I answered. It took an effort not to stutter. I was so cold that my teeth were beginning to chatter.

As Mitch Mahoney gazed at me, I studied him. He had died in Africa and I guessed that he was appearing before me at the age at which he'd met his end, just as Callum did. He was dressed in non-descript civvies, not the uniform he must have been wearing when he died. Yes, Mitch had filled out and his features had hardened, become more severe, despite the extra flesh clinging to his skull. His nose bent slightly to one side as though it had been broken and never reset. But some other change had been wrought in him that was unsettling, unnerving, something more than can be explained by maturity or that he was in fact dead.

For a start, his breath didn't frost the air as mine did. But that wasn't it. No, it was his eyes.

His gaze was fixed firmly upon my face but it seemed to be looking through me and beyond. The pupils were large; so large, and his face so fleshy, that the whites of his eyes were barely visible. Deep within the blackness, shadows shifted and changed like storm clouds in the night.

As I stared into those shifting depths, I felt as though I was toppling forward into the inky blackness. From somewhere, I heard a chuckle, a deep inhuman sound.

I tore my gaze away and immediately felt a sense of release. I swayed slightly and took a step back to steady myself.

The inhuman sound came again but this time in a snarl that would have sent shivers racing down my spine had I not already been freezing. I darted glances to each side but could not locate the source of the sound. There was only myself and Mitch in the Meadow and the sound hadn't come from him.

Mitch grunted and his shoulders sagged as if he'd been punched lightly in the stomach. Then he straightened and regarded me once more with an expression of sly cunning.

"You always were a slippery little bastard, Andrews," he remarked. "No matter. The Dead Lights will have you."

"There's no such thing as Dead Lights," I said.

I was careful not to stare into his eyes. Knowing now how a mouse must feel when hypnotised by a snake, I had no desire to repeat the experience.

"Ah, you'd know all about them, would you?" said Mitch. A sneer lifted his top lip. "You're nothing but a little shit who couldn't wipe his own arse without big brother by his side."

"What's happened to you, Mitch?" I asked quietly.

He snorted. "What, apart from dying you mean?"

I shook my head. "You were always a tough bastard and mean in a fight. But you weren't so nasty, so full of hatred. I even admired you, in a way."

He sneered again. "Then you're an even bigger dickhead than I thought."

"We're from the same place. Grew up on the same streets. I almost wept when I heard you'd been killed."

He was silent for a moment. A look of bitter reflection stole across his podgy features. When he spoke again, his voice was loaded with vitriol.

"War changes a man. I was in the Desert Rats. Know why we were called that? Because we died twitching and screaming in our own stinking guts and shit. Like rats in a trap."

"We won the war. Beat the Nazis. It wasn't in vain."

"Pah! Germans, Japs . . . makes no difference who won. Fucking Martians could have for all I care. Fight for your king and country? Die horribly for your king and country more like. Fuck 'em."

"It's made all the difference to those who are left. We—"

"Shut the fuck up! Your opinions are meaningless. Where I come from there's no race or nationalities, no politics, no wars. There's just. . . ."

"Just . . . ?"

"Shadows."

"Callum died in the war too. And Morfydd, my sister."

At the mention of my brother, an evil grin spread over Mitch's face like a rash.

"That *bastard*." He spat the word. "I've seen him in the shadows. Gonna bump into him soon and this time I'll not stop. No prissy little sister around to interfere." His expression became sly once more. It made my skin crawl. "By the way, Johnny, did you know that I fucked her before I joined the army? Slut begged me not to stop. Especially loved it up the arse. Just like her mother."

Although it was obvious that he was deliberately trying to provoke me, a red mist swam through my vision at his words. I fought to hold in my temper that was straining to fly free like a leaf in an autumn gale. I took a long deliberate breath of ice-cold air and held it in my lungs until the mist started to clear. When I spoke, I kept the anger hidden.

"Liked it up the arse did she, Mitch? Just like you, so I heard. 'Look out, boys, backs to the wall,' we'd say. 'Here comes Bum-boy Mahoney. No bending over—'"

I gasped in shock. Mitch had stepped forward and slapped me full across the cheek. He moved so quickly, like a striking cobra, I had no time to react. The left side of my head had gone completely numb.

Mitch stood toe to toe with me. Hs breath came in short, jerky spasms. Bright red spots showed lividly on his florid cheeks. Now that he was so close, I understood why his breath did not condense in the wintry air. The air that he exhaled into my face was cold, much colder than the air we breathed. It also stank. Dry-rot and dust, death and the grave. It made me want to gag.

I took a couple of steps backwards, more to get out of range of his breath than his fists. The skin of my left cheek sang as it slowly came back to life. Before long, it would be howling.

Mitch smirked. "Yellow to the core, just like your brother. Andrews brothers? More like the Andrews Sisters." He chuckled at his own wit.

I quickly sized up my situation. Mitch was clearly spoiling for a fight. I could look after myself but would be no match for the chuckling brute that stood before me. If Mitch charged, I would have to dodge and it would be like trying to avoid a raging bull. The grass was so frosty it would probably prove slippery underfoot. Once down, he would be on me like a felled oak. And there was no mercy lurking in the grim depths of Mitch's eyes.

The alternative was to run. To where, I had no clue; the horizon had the same featureless, hazy look in every direction. Yet it was a more attractive proposition than trying to fight him. So thinking, I turned my back on Mitch and took to my heels.

It *was* quite treacherous underfoot but, by not trying to run flat out, I managed to retain my balance. I also figured that unless Mitch had been transformed in the netherworld into the bulkiest sprinter ever seen, I could easily out-pace him at three-quarter speed.

His chuckles turned to raucous guffaws. But they did not recede as they should have as I put distance between us. He must be following me and keeping up easily, though I could not hear the thud of his feet pounding the frozen turf.

I slowed momentarily to risk a glance over my shoulder . . . and nearly fell over with fright. Mitch was no more than the two yards or so behind me that he had been when I started running. Yet he was still standing perfectly still. Still, that is, apart from the shaking caused by his merriment.

Increasing my speed as much as I dared, I did not look back again until I must have put fifty yards between us. His beaming face was still within touching distance. His legs were still planted firmly on the ground, unmoving.

Screaming silently in frustration, I continued to run but with my head craned backwards, keeping Mitch in view. He made no effort to set off after me but merely laughed all the harder until he was almost doubled up, hands on bended knees. But the distance between us increased and continued to increase with every step I took. The sound of his hilarity receded.

Conscious that I had no idea what I was running towards, I slowed my pace. But I dared not take my eyes from Mitch for a moment. Gradually, he grew smaller and smaller and his laughter became a distant murmur. My neck and back ached from the unnatural angle I had forced them into as I ran. At last, I could no longer see Mitch. All that lay behind me was a swathe of white spiky grass and a trail of footprints. With a huge sense of relief, I turned my head to face forwards.

I stopped dead in my tracks. The soles of my boots momentarily lost grip and I skidded to an ungainly halt. I almost ran headlong into Mitch.

He stood as I had left him, hands on knees, laughing so hard he would surely have been risking an embolism had he not already been dead. Tears of mirth rolled down his cheeks and froze. Tiny jewelled droplets collected above his jowls. He looked as though he'd been sneezed over by a snowman.

My breathing came hard and ragged. I felt as though I'd run two miles. Beads of perspiration rapidly cooled on my brow. I stared at Mitch in disbelief. Behind him, I could see the patches of green where he'd first stood before stepping forward to slap me. I glanced behind me and there were my footprints leading away. Alongside them was a similar set leading back to where I now stood.

As I caught my breath, Mitch's hysterics eased.

"Howay, man," he said. "That was the funniest thing I've seen in my life. Oops, in my *death* I should say." That set him off again.

I sighed. "Yeah, bloody hilarious. So—what happens now?"

As his laughter finally tailed away, he straightened, wiping at his eyes with an enormous fist.

"Now?" he said, his expression growing serious. "Now I kill you."

He lowered his arm and took a step towards me. A step more and I would be in range of those club-like fists.

I thought quickly. Mitch's expression and bearing said one thing: murder. I had tried running. All that remained was to fight. But how do you fight someone who is already dead?

Mitch took another step and a wild swipe that would have knocked me senseless had it connected. He was casual, confident in the knowledge that I did not possess the armoury to defeat him.

As I stepped easily out of range of the haymaker, I wondered what would happen to my earthly body that lay fast asleep in bed in Black Tops. Would it lie soulless and comatose until it expired of malnutrition or old age? Or would Ma try to wake me in the morning to find me already stiff and cold? Losing the last remaining member of her immediate family would surely destroy Ma. She had only just emerged from the despair of losing her husband.

The thought of Ma having to grieve yet again made me so angry that I stopped moving away from Mitch. Instead, and to his surprise, I stepped towards him and aimed a kick at his groin with all the force I could muster. He might have been surprised, but he was nevertheless too quick. With one huge fist, he cushioned the blow and thrust me backwards with contemptuous ease. I flailed, pinwheeling my arms for balance, and nearly fell. Had I done, it would have ended there for he was poised to pounce. When I managed to somehow stay upright, he merely shrugged and moved deliberately towards me, relentless as the tide.

He swung arcing, lazy punches that I dodged easily. When he tired of toying with me, I would be in serious trouble. I desperately tried to think of a way out, but all my mind could conjure was an image of Ma standing over my bed, head bowed, wringing her hands.

Mitch stopped swinging his arms. Holding his tightly-bunched fists slightly out from his body, he moved in for the kill.

My luck didn't hold. As I moved sharply to one side, my left foot slipped on the frosty grass. The only way to avoid doing the splits and rupturing my groin was to bring my other leg around, pitching me onto my back.

Mitch was onto me in a flash. The breath left my lungs with a *whumph!* as his bulk pinned me to the frozen ground. My arms were free but I could do little with them other than try to protect my face. Mitch grinned down on me in triumph.

"Got you now, you little shit," he spat. "It was nice knowing you. Bye bye."

Without further ado he laid into me. He punched my ears, pounded my head and pummelled my chest. I kept my arms across my face and he thumped those too. It was like being clubbed with a log. I bucked in a desperate attempt to throw him off, but I could not budge his dead weight. As the blows rained down, my consciousness began to waver. I could not survive much more, but Mitch showed no sign of relenting. I caught the occasional glimpse of his face. He grinned manically. Spittle fell from his lips.

My fading mind fixated on a picture of my sleeping self in bed at Black Tops. My sleeping self . . .

Of course. I was foolish not to have realised it sooner, almost fatally so. I lowered my arms from my face.

"No!" I shouted at Mitch with the last vestiges of my strength. "Stop! You can't hurt me."

He was taken aback enough at my outburst to stop punching for the moment. It took an effort, but I managed to lift my head a few inches off the ground so that I was closer to his round, stupid face.

"Do you hear me, Fat Boy?" I said. "You can't hurt me. Give up. Go home. Or to wherever the hell you come from."

A shadow of doubt passed across his features. Then he grinned. He raised his fists and clasped them together to form a lethal club. I stayed as I was, my head lifted unprotected towards him, my breathing short and harsh with the effort that took.

"Goodbye, Baby Andrews," said Mitch. "I'll be sure to tell big brother when I see him how you begged for your life, how you snivelled like a girl and how you shat your pants. Should be good for a few yuks."

Mitch tensed his wrists and brought his fists crashing down towards my face. I didn't flinch. If I was wrong, I would never know as the blow was delivered with such force that it would surely crush my skull and drive jagged shards of bone into my brain like shrapnel.

His aim was true. The fists landed squarely on the bridge of my nose.

Nothing happened.

Mitch stared incredulously, bushy eyebrows knitted together in confusion. He drew his right arm back and drove his fist into my face once more. Again his blow was true. Again I didn't feel a thing. My face remained intact.

I smiled and relaxed, allowing my head to fall back on the grass.

My expression did nothing to help Mitch's mood. He drew his arm back again and again, driving it down repeatedly to pound his knuckles into my unprotected face. By now it should have resembled freshly minced beef. It felt perfectly normal. I was cold—after all, I was lying on frosted grass—but I felt none of the blows. The aches, pains and numbness from the earlier beating had disappeared entirely.

Mitch was by now almost weeping with frustration. He continued pounding at my face, but he was tiring. There being nothing else I could do, I simply lay there and stared implacably at him, refusing to give him the satisfaction of even blinking at each ineffectual blow.

At last he gave up. He slid off me and slumped to the ground, breathing heavily.

I sat up. My sodden shirt clung icily to my back. It was my turn to gaze down at Mitch. He stared back at me uncomprehendingly. I almost felt pity for him. Almost.

"Do you get it, Mitch?" I asked, not really caring if he did or not.

"You can't hurt me here, in this place, wherever or whatever it is. You see, I'm not really here. I'm only dreaming that I'm here. At first, I dreamed that you were hurting me. I felt every blow. But as soon as I remembered that this is only a dream, from that moment you couldn't hurt me. Mind you, I only remembered in the nick of time. You almost had me."

Mitch had recovered some composure. His breathing had become less laboured and the stricken look had gone from his face. It had been replaced by the sullen expression of a thwarted bully.

"So it seems I can't kill you," he said. "There are others who will take care of that. But your beloved brother isn't part of any stupid dream. He's just as real as I am in the other place. He and I have unfinished business. What I couldn't do to you I'll do to him, only ten times worse."

A look of such smugness crept over his features that I started to wonder if it would work if I dreamed that *I* could hurt *him*. But then my shoulders sagged and my head bowed as a wave of utter exhaustion swept over me.

"Go away now, Mitch," I muttered. "I'm too tired. Go away. This is *my* dream, after all."

When I glanced back up, I wasn't surprised to see a large patch of flattened grass where Mitch had slumped. I looked quickly around to make sure he wasn't behind me. I was alone. Cold, wet, tired and alone.

I closed my eyes . . .

When I opened them again, I was lying on my bed in my bedroom. I put my hands to my face. Both hands and face were warm and none were sore. I was dressed once more in my nightshirt that bore no trace of dampness.

As I turned to my side to fall back to sleep, I became aware of a faint blue glow lighting the room. It was coming from outside through the uncurtained window.

Swimming

Darkness and the supernatural go together like hand and glove. Lying awake in the dead of night, listening to howling wind, creaking doors and the groans of a settling house, it is much easier to believe that ghosts exist than in the brightness of day. The dark cows our rationality and muffles our logic. It makes anything seem possible.

Following my meetings with Callum and the encounter with Mitch Mahoney in the Meadow, I formed a theory. Both my brother and Mitch inhabited a place that Callum called Darkland, a place of darkness and shadows. Suppose it is a place for recently-departed souls that have unfinished business with the living. Some of these souls may appear as spirits or ghosts in this world. But since they are accustomed to existing in darkness and shadow, perhaps (so my theory goes) they can only appear in this world under such conditions. They cannot exist in light.

It's only a theory but one that would help explain my experiences of the supernatural that occurred that summer. They all took place at night.

June slipped seamlessly into July. The weather became hotter and drier, the days longer. Britain baked.

On the day that I next saw Mary the sun beamed down from a sky that was completely devoid of moisture, like some vast blue desert.

The air was still, not generating so much as a sigh to cool beaded brows.

I trudged from the village, passing through clouds of midges that flocked along the stream. They feasted gloriously on the copious amounts of sweat pouring from every pore in my body.

Arriving at the Glade, I flung myself headlong by the stream and thrust my face beneath the babbling surface. The startling coldness of the water made my cheeks tingle as it washed away perspiration and squashed gnats. I held my face under for as long as I could hold my breath. After surfacing briefly, panting and spluttering, I plunged my whole head beneath the surface. I repeated the process, only stopping when the iciness made my head pound. An onlooker would have thought I'd gone nuts or was making an ineffectual attempt at drowning myself.

I stumbled up the slope and flopped down in the shade of the trees. Deliciously cool droplets ran down my back and chest. Within minutes, despite being out of the direct glare of the sun, my thick hair had dried and I was perspiring anew.

When Mary ambled into the Glade my eyes were starting to close as a nap beckoned, but I snapped back to full alertness at the sight of her.

She came not from the direction of the village but from the woods on the other side of the stream. She had made some wildflowers into a chain that she wore on her head, like a garland or coronet fit for a wood goddess.

Her face lit up in a smile when she saw me. My heart instantly began to pump harder and fresh beads of sweat popped onto my brow.

She flopped down beside me. She had her own beads of perspiration along her nose and lightly dotting her cheeks.

"It's so hot," she sighed.

"Aye," I agreed, unable to tear my gaze away from her. "What are you up to?"

"Been for a walk, but it's too hot to go far. I just needed to get away for a while."

"Away from your father?"

She nodded. "He's not in a good mood today. This heat is making him more irritable than ever. I could see the warning signs and got out before. . . ."

"Before what?" I asked gently. "Does he hit you?"

She grimaced. "Sometimes," she said. "But he doesn't mean to hurt me. He's always sorry afterwards."

I looked away and bit my lip. I didn't think that sharing my thoughts on fathers who beat their daughters would really help much. And I didn't want to risk driving her off and lose the opportunity of spending the rest of the day with her. Maybe I needed to lighten the mood.

I stood and executed a clumsy bow. "Would my Lady care to accompany me on an afternoon's stroll this fine day?" I spoke in a hopeless attempt at what I imagined was an aristocratic accent and doffed an imaginary feathered cap.

Mary smiled and answered in a passable approximation of an English country lady. "One would be honoured, young Sir. But the intense heat doth make one quite faint. Where would young Sir propose to promenade?"

"Umm. . . ." I didn't know what else to say. She was better at this than me.

"One would much desire to partake of the land's end where salty breezes disturb the air and set a lady's heart aflutter."

"Er, you want to go to the beach?"

She grinned and dropped the plummy accent. "I certainly do. It's always cooler there."

I held out my hand and yanked her to her feet. Her breasts pressed tightly against her blouse. I averted my gaze, perhaps too obviously for I became aware from the corner of my eye that she was considering me.

I ambled off nonchalantly in the direction of the sea, hoping that in all the heat and sweat she wouldn't notice the sudden reddening of my neck. After a pause, Mary followed.

We traced the path of the stream to the coast. By the time we were in sight of the sea, we were both bathed in a sheen of perspiration. Had I been a dog, my tongue would have been scraping the ground.

At a point where the stream narrowed, Mary jumped lithely across to the other side.

"Come on," she called. "There's a sandy beach this way."

I sprang across after her, spraying droplets of sweat as I landed.

Mary glanced back with a look of devilment. Kicking off her shoes, she ran lightly away across the heather, giggling like an excited child.

I picked up her shoes and broke into a lumbering run. It didn't last long—it was way too hot to run—and I soon slowed to a gentle walk. Sweat ran freely into my eyes and my boots felt as though they were lined with lead. The light breeze that blew from the sea did little to cool me down. I plodded along after Mary, grumbling to myself.

She had taken off like a startled gazelle and had quickly gone from sight. I had not been in this direction during my previous explorations, but reasoned that so long as I stayed near the cliff edge I couldn't miss her.

Before I had gone far, the cliffs dropped to meet the beach at a point where there must have been another fold of softer rock, rising quickly again the other side. As I approached the cleft, I could see the golden glimmer of sand.

The sand formed a crescent bay, bounded by rocky outcrops at either end, and shelved unbroken to the sea a hundred yards away. The tide must have been out for a while because the sand at the base of the cleft was bone dry. I trudged along it, feet sinking almost to the ankles, looking for Mary. As I sat down to remove my boots, I saw her. She was in the sea.

Leaving my boots and Mary's shoes where I'd sat, I walked towards the water. At first, the sand was so hot against the soles of my feet that I almost had to scurry to make it bearable. But as I approached the water's edge, the surface grew cooler and firmer and I was able to resume my normal gait.

A pile of some sort of material caught my attention and I deviated towards it. It was only when I was upon it that I recognised the pile as Mary's clothes. I could make out her blouse and long skirt. A white stiff-looking contraption I assumed to be her bra. Her knickers were white, too, and lay carelessly on top of the pile like a lowered flag of truce.

I gulped, suddenly finding it difficult to breathe. Tearing my gaze away from the pile of clothes, I continued down to the water's edge. *Oh my God she's naked, oh my God she's naked* played over and over in my mind. I kept my head down, afraid to look up, dying to look up. I could hear Mary splashing and uttering whoops of joy. When I reached the lapping water I halted, head still lowered, toes digging into the cool wet sand.

"Come on in, John. It's wonderful!"

I risked a glance up. The sea was in that calm stage, the slack period, before the tide turns and barely a ripple disturbed the surface of the clear waters. Mary was about fifteen yards from where I stood, up to her shoulders in water. This I noted with both relief and disappointment. The water had turned her hair black and sleek, and it glistened in the sunlight like the hide of a seal. As she maintained her balance in the gentle swell by languidly swaying her forearms to either side, as though conducting a choir, I could make out the white curves of her breasts beneath the shimmering surface. I gulped hard again.

"Come on," she called. "What are you waiting for?"

She brought one arm out of the water and slapped it down on the surface to send a spray of salty droplets towards me. For one fantastic moment, all the colours of the spectrum came curving through the air. The sight of hundreds of miniature flying rainbows would have delighted me if it hadn't been overshadowed by a more amazing spectacle. As Mary had raised her arm free of the water, her upper torso made a brief appearance. It was only the shortest of glimpses, but the view imprinted in my mind like a photograph. Her breasts looked as firm and perfectly formed as I had imagined. The nipples had hardened in the cool of the water and pointed at me tauntingly before dipping back below the surface.

This time I gulped so hard my Adam's apple must have reached my toes.

"Come *on*!" She chuckled throatily; almost a growl. "Get your clothes off!"

A sick feeling started to form just below my sternum. It had little to do with the glimpse of Mary's breasts. A lot more to do with her trying to cajole me into the water.

She called again, a trace of annoyance creeping into her tone. I knew that I would have to come clean and the sick feeling expanded.

"I can't," I said in a small voice.

"What did you say?"

"I can't come in," I said, a little louder. I took another gulp of air, trying to force the nausea down.

Mary swam towards me until she was less than five yards from the shore. She was now in shallower water and kept her body beneath the surface by placing her hands on the sandy seabed as support for her body that she stretched out behind her. I could see her breasts clearly now, distorted by refraction but nonetheless delectable. The sickness that had come upon me prevented me from fully enjoying the view.

"What's wrong, John?" She was regarding me with some concern. "Are you feeling all right? You look a little ill."

I swallowed hard again. "I'm fine," I muttered.

"Then why don't you come for a dip? It's so cool in here."

"Look, I just can't, okay?"

"But *why*? If it's your body, I promise I won't look."

"It's not that."

"Some rare skin disease?"

"*No*!" She was determined to wring it out of me, but some stubbornness or pride kept me from coming out with it. I cast my gaze down at my feet and breathed deeply, trying to dispel the nausea.

"All right, then," said Mary. "You must be an escaped circus freak. No sexual organs. 'Roll up, roll up. Come and see the Amazing Dickless Wonder. Man or woman? You decide. How does it pee? Come inside and see!'" She broke off into helpless giggles.

"Ha ha, very funny." I sighed, knowing there was no escape. "Look, the reason I can't come in the sea is. . . ."

"Yes, Dickless?"

"Ah, shit! Right . . . *I can't swim*. There, I've said it. Happy now?" I stared even harder at my toes and dug them savagely into the sand. At least now the admission was out, the sick feeling had already started to pass.

"Oh," said Mary. I glanced at her. She was trying hard, but not very successfully, to hide her amusement. "Never mind," she said. "You can still paddle. Be careful though. The bottom slopes steeply a few yards in. I'm going to have a quick swim, then I'll be out."

She turned and swam smoothly away from shore. I watched her go, my pride hurt. I was the big, strong City Boy . . . who couldn't swim.

I took a few backward steps up the beach. Mary was still swimming away from me, black head bobbing above the gentle swell.

How difficult can it be? I thought. *Children of three learn how to swim.*

I stripped off my clothes to my underpants. For a moment I hesitated, then shrugged them off as well. I took a deep breath and ran.

With a shrill holler of bravado, I flung myself headfirst into the sea. Things then became rather confused.

The water was shockingly cold. It ripped the air from my lungs like a burst balloon. Too late I realised that it might have been a good idea to close my mouth. Foul salt water rushed down my throat. As I tried to gag it back up, more found its way in. My world abruptly became a swirling maelstrom of blues and greens, dancing to the sounds of blood pounding in my ears, whooshing of bubbles and my desperate, echoing, suffocated cries.

My head thudded into something soft and gritty. I thrashed my arms and kicked my legs, not knowing up from down, left from right. I wasn't only panicking: I was drowning.

A sharp tug to my head made me yelp in pain. More brackish water rushed into my already saturated body. Then the sun was shining in my face as my head broke the surface.

I coughed and spluttered, expelling water from my lungs and stomach, along with breakfast and lunch. Mary let go of my hair and smartly retreated a safe distance. Her chest must have been fully exposed, but I was in no condition to notice. I stood in water that barely reached above my waist, creating a slick of vomit. I had very nearly managed to drown in less than four feet of water.

After what seemed an eternity, but was probably less than a minute, my retching eased and I gulped in great mouthfuls of sweet, sweet air. Breathing had never felt so good.

I glanced at Mary. She crouched in the water, a complicated mixture of amusement, annoyance and, which pleased me, concern etched on her features.

"Thanks," I managed to splutter in between gulps.

"Idiot!" she exclaimed. "You could have drowned."

"Sorry," I mumbled.

"Men! Always have to prove that nothing's beyond them, even when it so obviously is."

I cast my gaze down. My feet shimmered whitely beneath me like two plucked ducks.

"I'm getting out now," said Mary. "Please turn your head away."

For want of anything better to do as Mary splashed out of the sea behind me, I studied the dispersing slick of vomit, trying to identify partially-digested items of food.

"I'm dressed. You can turn around now."

She was standing on the sand, hands on hips, next to my pile of clothes. I trudged out of the water. It was only when I stood dripping in front of her that I remembered I was completely naked. I flung my hands in front of me to cover my embarrassment.

Mary raised one eyebrow. At least the annoyance had left her face.

"Hmm," she murmured. "I was obviously *very* wrong when I said you had no sexual organs." She leaned quickly forward and planted a kiss full on my lips. "I'll be in the glade the afternoon after tomorrow." She swirled round and walked away, not looking back.

I stood watching her go, thinking about her kiss. It had been too brief for me to taste anything but salt on her lips. Bearing in mind what had very recently passed between *my* lips, I hoped fervently that it was only salt she'd been able to taste on mine.

The heat of the sun quickly dried my skin. I dressed in a daze. Apart from a dull ache in my ribs and a mild sore throat, I had recovered from my underwater adventure but I could not get that kiss, and the promise of more that lay behind it, out of my thoughts.

Despite the cooling dip in the sea, I was soon sweating freely again as I trudged back to the village. My shirt prickled uncomfortably against my salt-encrusted skin.

But the heat could do nothing to sap my spirit. It soared even as my body wilted. She had kissed me and I would be seeing her again in two days' time.

That night, though, something happened that drove my excitement away in a rush of terror.

An Unwelcome Visitor

It had been the hottest day so far in a summer brimming with hot days. The thick stone walls of Black Tops helped keep the interior cooler than the temperature outside, but it was still warm in my bedroom. I opened the windows to their fullest extent before retiring to bed that evening of my trip to the beach with Mary. I fell asleep with only a sheet covering me to the waist, the rest of the bedclothes crumpled at the foot of the bed.

Yet, when I awoke I was cold.

My body clock told me that the hour was early but it was difficult to be certain due to the blue glow that bathed the room in an eerie translucence. The Dead Lights were abroad.

I came to lying on my right side, my face at the edge of the double bed. My back was cold. Barely half awake, I reached down and tugged the sheet up to my shoulders. My back remained cold, though the front of my body was warm, uncomfortably so. The air in the room was almost as stiflingly hot as when I'd gone to bed.

With a start, I realised that the source of the coldness was behind me. I awoke fully and started to turn over. That was when I heard the sound of breathing and knew I was not alone.

I froze in mid turn. A deep chill seeped into my left side as though I lay next to a block of ice.

The breathing came from that side. Ragged and wet. It reminded me of the tortured sounds of Da's breathing in his final hours when he fought unsuccessfully against double pneumonia.

Then I noticed the smell. The pond in the field behind Black Tops had started to give off the same unpleasant aroma. As the water level receded in the merciless glare of the sun, the remaining brown sludge had started to emit a pungent whiff like a mixture of rotting vegetation and sewage. The smell emanating from my left was the same, but stronger. The stink of bog, of marsh gases, of decay and death. Had I not been completely immobilised with fear, I'm sure I would have vomited for the second time in twenty-four hours.

I must have lain on my back, unmoving, for only a matter of seconds, but it felt like minutes passed while I struggled to make my limbs move, get up, flee from whatever shared my bed.

Not knowing what lay beside me was worse than knowing, and eventually broke my paralysis. I turned my head fully to the left.

The blue glow of the Dead Lights provided enough illumination to enable me to see clearly—far too clearly—my unbidden bed fellow.

It was a girl, or something resembling a girl, lying on her back, head turned towards me.

One eyeball regarded me with calm malevolence. It was covered in a pearly film, like the rheumy eyes of Old Joe in the village shop. Beneath the film, a red point sparked like a flaring ember. The other socket was eyeless. It was filled instead by a pit of utter blackness.

The skin covering the face was flaccid and wrinkled, and white as the belly of a fish. The skin on my fingers wrinkles like that if I dwell too long in the bath.

The hair straggling the face was brown, lank and wet. Strands of weed tangled within. One frond hung limply down the forehead like a sickly green lock of hair.

Lips resembling two bloated, pale-pink worms parted and small gusts of foul, chilled air wafted into my face as the thing wheezed.

For a moment I could do nothing but stare into the face. I don't know how, but I managed to prevent my bladder letting go in a hot rush. From somewhere that seemed far away I became aware of a pitiful whimpering, before realising that the sound came from my throat.

The creature's pallid lips pulled back to reveal crooked brown teeth and gums that looked as pale and slimy as the surface of a sweating mushroom. I couldn't tell if it was grinning or grimacing. Then the thing spoke.

"Jo—hn . . . come to me. . . ." A deathly whisper that reached my ears on a draught of charnel house air.

I stared transfixed as the creature lifted its left arm and brought its hand slowly towards my cheek. The skin of the hand was white and dead like skin around a cut that has spent too long hidden beneath a plaster. The fingernails were long and tapering and yellow like a heavy smoker's. Fingers curled slightly inwards, claw-like. The flesh of my cheek crawled with revulsion as the hand drew nearer, but still I was powerless to act. Cold fingers touched my right cheek, stroking it almost tenderly.

An icy void opened within my flesh beneath the thing's caress. It started to spread inside my head, making for the brain. Had it reached it, I have no doubt that Ma would have come to wake me in the morning to find me dead, stiff and cold, extremely cold.

Once again, as it had in the Meadow under the onslaught of Mitch Mahoney, it was the thought of Ma losing her only remaining child that saved me.

I opened my mouth and uttered the loudest noise that I was capable of making. Whether a shout or scream, I'm not sure, but it was sufficient to break my paralysis. Still yelling or screaming, I jerked my head backwards in disgust, dislodging the creature's hand from my cheek. Immediately, the icy pressure that had been building inside my skull lessened.

The creature hissed like an angry cobra. Its one eye flared a deep scarlet that momentarily obscured the milky cataract. It reached out its hand to me again, quicker this time, but I was already on the move, scrabbling wildly backwards.

The hand missed my face by a whisker. I felt the searing chill of its passage across my cheeks and nose. The hand hit the bed, talon-like fingernails snagging in the bedsheet. The creature dug its fingers in further and started to pull itself towards me.

I lurched off the edge of the bed and thudded heavily to the floor where I lay on my back, winded and momentarily silenced. Yellowing, curled fingernails appeared over the lip of the bed and a fresh jolt of sickening terror sliced into me as I realised that the creature would in moments drag itself over the edge and drop onto me.

Struggling to get air into my lungs, I tried to scrabble sideways but could gain no purchase on the polished wooden floorboards. The creature's arm was now dangling over the bed, grasping at the mattress to pull the creature over.

A commotion came from my right as the bedroom door burst open and flickering light from an oil lamp flooded the room, banishing the blue glow of the Dead Lights. I turned in that direction and managed to roll away from the bed as at last I was able to gasp in a lungful of air.

Ma stood in the open doorway, holding a lamp in one hand, the other clutching the throat of her nightdress in concern.

I screamed up at her, "Ma, on the bed! Don't go near it . . . the bed!" I scrambled sideways until I reached her and clutched desperately at the hem of her nightie, all the while screaming at her not to go near the bed.

Then she was crouching, her arms encircling my trembling body.

"Hush, Johnny, hush. It's all right now. It was just a dream. There's nothing there. Look."

She stood and raised the lamp. I rose shakily to my knees and looked at the bed, ready to spring to my feet and run, dragging Ma with me. There was no need. Ma was right. There was nothing there except a bed and crumpled sheets.

A deep surge of relief swelled within, threatening to overwhelm me. I steeled myself against it. I had to be sure.

I rose unsteadily to my feet and took the lamp from Ma, silencing her question with a curt shake of my head. The sheet that had covered me was rucked and askew, but nothing was concealed beneath it. I walked gingerly around to the edge of the bed, still poised to take flight. Cautiously, I lowered the lamp and peeked around the far side of the bed. There was nothing on the floor. Moving more purposefully now, I strode to the windows and looked down and up. Nothing was crawling down the walls or slinking across the garden as far as I could see. The garden was in darkness: the Dead Lights had gone out. Finally I returned to the bed, crouched and placed the lamp on the floor. I peered under the bed. Nothing there except dust.

Satisfied that the thing had really gone, I allowed myself to relax. I handed the lamp back to Ma with a small smile and sat on the edge of the bed. I was still trembling but now it was due to reaction, not to the fright itself.

Then I started. A white face was peering around the door.

"Everything all right?" asked Gwen.

"Aye," said Ma. "He's been having a nightmare."

Gwen came into the room. "Nightmare, eh? Nasty things. You sounded as though all the hounds of hell were after you." She looked piercingly at me.

I forced a light chuckle. "Aye, something like that. But it was just a dream."

"Hmm," said Gwen. "Well, I'm glad it's over. I'll see you in the morning." She ruffled my hair and gave her sister a peck on the cheek before leaving.

Ma's expression was still one of concern. She sat next to me on the bed. "It *was* just a nightmare, John, wasn't it?"

"Of course it was. What else could it have been?"

She shook her head, but the worried look remained.

"I'm all right now," I said. "Go back to bed."

"Well . . . if you're sure," she said. "I suppose you're a big boy now and can look after yourself." She paused. "Can I ask a favour, John?"

"Of course you can."

"Promise me that you will be very careful."

"What do you mean, Ma?"

"Never mind what I mean. Just promise me that you will be very careful. Go on, promise."

"Okay. I promise I'll be very careful. But—"

"No buts. And another thing. Wear Callum's St Christopher. Don't look at me like that, young man!" Her tone softened. "Look, *cariad*, don't ask questions. Just do this one thing to make an old woman happy. From now on, wear Callum's medallion all the time, wherever you go. Please."

"I suppose . . . yeah, all right."

She hugged me, almost fiercely. I hugged her back. Then I took her lamp and used it to light the small lamp that was kept in my bedroom. I didn't fancy spending what remained of the night in darkness. I doubted that sleep would come easily, if at all. To lie awake in the dark, straining my ears for the sound of someone, or something, breathing was not a prospect that filled me with joy.

Ma went back to bed, closing my bedroom door softly behind her. I walked around the bed to the small cabinet where I kept the box of items that had belonged to my brother. I opened it and withdrew the St Christopher. It had tarnished a little over the years, but still glinted softly in the lamp light. My trembling had eased, so I had little difficulty in tying the medallion around my neck on the silver chain—the clasp was, of course, broken after being tugged from my dying brother's neck by his friend, Private Black. I tucked it inside my nightshirt where its coldness against my chest was oddly comforting.

I turned the lamp's wick down low and left the lamp on the cabinet. It cast sufficient light to keep the deepest shadows at bay. I lay back on the right side of the bed, pulling the sheet over my legs and up to my waist.

Sleep eluded me as I thought it might. I could not help but keep glancing to my left to where it had been lying. There was no physical evidence to show it had really been there: no indentation in the mattress, no tears in the bottom sheet where its talons had snagged, no after-odour of rotting vegetation. Maybe it had, after all, been a particularly vivid dream.

On impulse, I stretched out my left arm and lay it on the sheet where the creature had lain. The balmy air has begun to warm it back up, but there was no question about it. The sheet was icily cold.

Ma's expression was still troubled the following morning. She and Gwen fussed over me at breakfast like mother hens. I assured them that I was fine and that I had merely experienced a particularly scary nightmare.

The fear I'd experienced in the night had largely been replaced by a curiosity and determination to try to discover who or what my night-time visitor was and why she or it had paid me a visit. I didn't believe it had been a social call.

"Auntie Gwen," I began, "have you heard any stories, *real* stories about the village?"

"What sort of stories, love?"

"Oh, any really. Particularly about things that happened a long time ago, perhaps before you came here."

Gwen thought for a moment. "Well . . . I did hear something once about a family that lived in these parts. Apparently something happened to them that was out of the ordinary."

"Yes?" I leaned forward in my chair, eager to hear more.

"That's about all I know. I've never had that much interest in what goes on around here. And I was only told part of the story. Someone—hmm I think it was Frank Fletcher—interrupted as if he didn't want the story aired."

My disappointment must have shown in my face, for Gwen continued: "Why don't you ask Mr Bailey about it? I think it was him who told me about the family. Yes, it must have been him. We were on our way to market."

"Who's Mr Bailey? Does he live around here?"

"Oh yes. You've met him."

"I have?" The only male villagers I could recall meeting were the inn-keeper's son and the gummy, rheumy old man in the shop. "Oh, you don't mean that old man Joe, do you?"

"No, no," said Gwen with a laugh. "That grumpy old so-and-so wouldn't pass a civil word with anyone, least of all me. No, Mr Bailey is the farmer who gave you a lift on his cart."

I thought back to our arrival in Tregeagle, bumping along the lane on the back of the cart. The cart's owner had seemed friendly enough. In comparison to most of the villagers I'd since met, he had been positively gushing with conviviality.

"His farm lies beyond the village, further down the lane, doesn't it?" I asked.

"Aye. The lane ends at the farm. Why, love, going to pay him a visit? If you are, you can pick up a pound of butter. There's some early rhubarb you can take him in exchange. Loves making rhubarb tart does Mrs Bailey."

I nodded. Yes, why not pay a visit to farmer Bailey?

Ma was looking at me, a frown furrowing her brow. I smiled to reassure her. I dipped my hand inside my shirt and flashed the St Christopher medallion. Ma returned my smile, but it looked weak and forced.

The Farmer's Tale

The village was deserted as usual as I strolled through later that morning, a bunch of rhubarb sticks wrapped in brown paper tucked comfortably under one arm.

A gentle breeze made it more pleasant than the previous day's unrelenting heat.

As I passed beyond the village and the birds began to sing, the last of my fears dissipated and I whistled along with the birds as I sauntered up the lane.

The lane was bounded to my right by a continuous drystone wall that ran its entire remaining length, roughly two miles. The forest that grew behind Tregeagle, now unchecked by buildings and gardens, crept right up to the wall where trees jostled together, boughs entwined, like spindly green giants. By walking close to the wall, the trees provided sufficient shade to prevent the hike becoming arduous.

The other side of the lane, the coastal side, was bounded by hedgerow with fields beyond. The lane acted as a buffer between these contrasting landscapes. To my left lay green open space, to my right thick woody denseness. The lane curved gently between them as though keeping two naughty children apart.

I smelled the farm before I saw it. Some people wax lyrical about the healthy smell of the countryside. To me, it just smelled like cowshit.

Gwen had been right about the lane ending at the farm. As I approached, the wall sloped away to my right, taking the forest with it. The hedge to my left broke away at a right angle. The lane simply petered out and became a farmyard.

The yard consisted of little more than dust and pebbles that would no doubt become a muddy quagmire in wet weather. A flagstone path ran from the end of the lane to the farmhouse to provide a less muddy means of access in winter. A few chickens pecked half-heartedly at the dust watched over by a strutting cockerel whose crown looked to be wilting in the late morning sunshine.

A low whitewashed building stood to my left, a barn and a few other outbuildings to my right, together loosely forming two sides of a courtyard. The farmhouse lay straight ahead, an imposing stone edifice that looked as if it had been built to last.

As I stood wondering whether to shout or walk to the front door and knock, a sheepdog came panting around the side of the house, closely followed by a young child. The child, a boy of about three at a guess, stopped uncertainly when he spotted me. The dog came bounding up, tail wagging so hard it raised small billows of dust in its wake. The dog lifted its forepaws and planted them firmly in my midriff. It grinned up at me, vivid pink tongue dangling as if only joined by a thread and dripping like the roof of a cave. I ruffled its floppy ears and tried to keep the package of rhubarb away from its tongue.

While I fussed the dog, the young boy had approached to within a few yards. He regarded me with wide eyes, one thumb inserted securely in his mouth. I smiled at him.

"Hello," I said. "I'm John. What's your name?"

"Puh-buh," it sounded like. It might have helped if he'd removed the thumb before speaking.

"Are your father and mother home?" Then realising that he was probably too young to be Mr Bailey's son, I added: "Or your granddad?"

This time his reply was completely unintelligible. He stood and stared at me, thumb moving in and out like a piston. Meanwhile, the dog showed no sign of moving. Its tongue continued to drip copiously, saturating my shirt. I moved my hand away from its ears but it did not take the hint. It tried instead to lick my face, straining its head upwards and discharging a fresh volley of spittle in all directions, so that I hurriedly resumed rubbing its ears. I guessed it was not the farm's guard dog.

Goodness knows how long I would have stood like that had not a voice boomed out, "Get down Shep!"

The dog complied with the order at once, dropping to the ground where it sat on its haunches and panted.

Startled but thankfully free of dog, I glanced around to find the owner of the voice. It belonged to a man in his late twenties who was eyeing me with some suspicion as he approached.

"Hi," I said in what I hoped was a disarming tone. "I've come from the village. My name's John Andrews. Is Mr Bailey about?"

"John Andrews? Not heard that name before." He stopped in front of me, next to the child who held up his free hand and grasped one of the man's.

"No," I said. "I've only been in the village since May. Me and my mother are staying with her sister, Gwen Evans."

At the mention of Gwen's name, his bearing seemed to relax. "I've met Gwen. Nice lady. Welsh ain't she?"

"Aye. Me Ma too."

"Not you though by the sound of it. From up north?"

"Aye. Newcastle born and bred."

"Ah, the place with the shite football team." I immediately started to bristle, until I noticed the wide grin that lit up his face. He released the child's hand and stepped forward to shake mine. "Only joshing you, lad. The Magpies ain't a bad side. I'm a John too—John Oakes."

I gripped his hand and returned the smile. He turned to the child.

"Peter, go fetch Gramps." He looked at the dog. "Git Shep." The dog bounded away and disappeared from view. I was glad to see the back of it.

John turned back to me. "I'm Arthur Bailey's son-in-law. One of them anyhow. Sorry if I seemed stand-offish. We don't often get strangers out this way."

"S'okay," I replied. "So what team do you support?"

We spent the next few minutes chatting about football. I had missed talking with someone knowledgeable about the game. It was no good trying to talk football with Ma and Gwen. They simply didn't have the passion.

Our conversation was interrupted by the arrival of Arthur Bailey. He came from the side of the house, wiping his hands on a cloth. His ruddy features lit up in a smile of recognition and he engulfed my hand in a huge fist.

"Gwen Evans's nephew if I'm not mistaken," he said.

"Hello, sir. John Andrews. Auntie Gwen sent me for a pound of butter. I've brought this in exchange." I held out the parcel of rhubarb. The feathery ends of the stalks were starting to look a little worse for wear.

The farmer took the parcel. "This'll do nicely. Your aunt's rhubarb is the best around. My wife will turn this into a delicious tart." Arthur Bailey was probably in his fifties, stocky and fit-looking. His eyes twinkled as he surveyed the parcel. "Splendid! I'll just get these stalks into the kitchen before they wilt any more in this heat. John here will sort you out with the butter. Nice to see you again." He turned to go.

"Er, actually, sir, I thought we might have a chat. If you've got a minute or two to spare. . . ."

He turned back and favoured me with a keen glance, green eyes still twinkling beneath bushy, sandy eyebrows. "Come round to the kitchen, at the back of the house, when you've got your butter. I was just about to have five minutes with a glass of scrumpy. You look like you could do with a cool drink yourself."

"Aye, sir. I certainly could."

"Splendid! By the way, the name's Arthur. Hadn't been knighted last I noticed."

The dairy was housed in the low white building. The interior was dim and deliciously cool after the glaring heat of the yard. John Oakes bustled away in the back, before returning with the butter. The creamy yellow lump was ensconced in a heavy earthenware pot that was oddly shaped, curved like a vase and seeming far too big for just a pound of butter. The reason for the extra size soon became apparent. The butter compartment was surrounded on all sides, except above, by a two inch gap. There was a hole in the rim into which John carefully ladled cold water from a large churn, filling the gap to the brim. He then sealed the pot with a heavy lid and handed it to me. It was quite a load.

"There you go," he said. "It's not ideal but that should prevent the butter melting too much on your way back. Don't tarry and get it straight into the larder when you get home."

"Thank you," I said. "What about the container?"

"Your aunt can drop it at the store and we'll pick it up next time we make a delivery. Best leave it in the cool here for now. Just pop in and collect it on your way out." He took the pot from me and placed it on a rough wooden table.

"Right. Thanks. See you again."

"Next time you're up this way, when it's not so hot, there's an old football around here somewhere. We could have a kickabout."

"That would be great." I meant it too. I hadn't kicked a ball since we left Newcastle. When you are raised in that city, football is in your blood and I longed to have a ball at my feet once more.

John accompanied me outside and headed for the barn while I made my way around the side of the house to the rear entrance.

Ducks, geese and more chickens waddled, honked and pecked their way around the dusty rear yard and the large garden that lay beyond. Further on, I could see vast chequered fields most of which were occupied by black and white or brown cows. One or two fields appeared to be devoted to crops.

A couple of goats chewed at the grass that covered half the garden. The other half was given to vegetables. A crude wooden stake fence served to keep the goats out of the vegetable patch. Some lambs, sturdy looking creatures rather than the fragile bundles I'd imagined them to be, gambolled and annoyed the goats. A half-full washing line ran the length of the garden, clothes swaying in the gentle breeze.

The young boy Peter sat on the grass playing with a toy, seemingly unconcerned by the munching goats and frisky lambs. His thumb was still planted firmly in his mouth. As I smiled at Peter, I idly wondered what his thumb would look like if he ever pulled it from his mouth. At once an image of the pale, flaccid skin of the girl who had paid me an unbidden visit in the night popped into my mind. With a shudder, I turned towards the farmhouse.

The back door was in two sections. The bottom half was closed against the poultry while the top half was thrown wide to allow the breeze to enter the house. I had never seen such a door before. As I stared, the top portion of a person appeared in the gap. It was a woman, short and plump with fair curly hair and the same ruddy complexion as Arthur Bailey's.

The chubby face broke into a smile at seeing me. Deep dimples appeared either side of her mouth and I found myself taking an instant liking to her.

"You must be John," she said. "Come in, come in." She opened the bottom half of the door and held it while I walked past, closing it immediately behind me. "Must keep the door shut. Pesky chickens will be in otherwise the moment my back's turned."

I found myself in an enormous room. It was obviously the focal point of the house and served as more than just a kitchen. A vast range occupied nearly the whole of one wall, a large vat of liquid boiling merrily away on the hob. Yet the room was not as hot as I would have expected. Its vastness, thick stone walls and breeze all combined to make the temperature pleasantly cool.

An ancient wooden table took up the centre of the flagstoned floor. A dozen chairs stood around it. Only one was currently occupied. Arthur Bailey sat at the table, sipping from a tankard.

"Grab yourself a chair, John," he said. "Drop of scrumpy suit you?"

"Yes please, si—I mean, Arthur."

I pulled out a chair and sat down. Mrs Bailey placed a large mug of cool cider in front of me. It was a potent brew and I only sipped at it, too aware of the long walk back to Tregeagle that faced me. Mrs Bailey, or Ida as she insisted I call her, bustled about the kitchen throwing in her own comments here and there as her husband chatted about his farm and extended family.

Arthur stood to refill his tankard from the demi-john that stood on a work surface. As he sat back down, he said, "So what did you want to ask me about?"

"Well, I'd like to find out a little of the history of Tregeagle. My aunt has lived there for years but knows nothing of its past."

"That doesn't surprise me," said Arthur. "Not very inquisitive is she, your aunt? Very untypical of a woman." He winked at me and grinned at his wife who stuck her tongue out in mock anger. "What in particular do you want to know?"

I wondered briefly whether to plunge straight in and ask about previous occupants of Black Tops, but decided it might be wiser for now to confine my questions to more general matters.

"Well, anything really," I said lamely.

"I could talk for hours about the village's history," said Arthur. "My father was a bit of an amateur historian and passed the interest down to me. This farm was built by my great-grandfather, which makes me the fourth generation Bailey to raise a family here. When me and Ida have gone, there'll be no Baileys living here for the first time in over a hundred years. No sons and two married daughters, see," he said in answer to my raised eyebrow.

He paused for a deep draught of cider then went on: "Tregeagle grew to its current size about seventy years ago. Its population increased tenfold in a little over two years. A tin lode was discovered to the north of what was then only a handful of crofters' cottages. Word got out and people poured in, hoping to make a killing from mining the tin. And they did make money. Enough to build cottages, a church, the pub, the shop. They made grand plans to extend the village into a town and build roads to connect to other towns and cities. There was even talk of a railway line. Your aunt's house, Black Tops, was built by a man called Harold Sedgwick who was credited with first discovering the mine. The Sedgwick family still owns the house, I believe, although they have not lived in the village for over sixty years.

"My father remembered the time well. He said that the villagers were full of grand ideas as to how they would use their wealth to make Tregeagle one of the most important towns in the Southwest. But, as you can tell, their grand schemes came to naught." He paused again to wet his whistle before continuing.

"You see, they forgot to check one important thing. How long would the tin last? Nobody thought to have the lode surveyed to gauge its extent. Within two years, the tin ran out. Within another year, half of the newly-expanded population had upped sticks and left. With the mine exhausted there was no reason for them to stay. And I believe that some were driven out. A lot of cottages have stood empty for years. Some of the remaining inhabitants must carry out routine maintenance to the empty buildings from time to time. Otherwise they'd have fallen to ruin by now."

"Why should they do that?" I asked. "The villagers that I've met don't strike me as taking any particular pride in their surroundings. Not enough to repair cottages that don't even belong to them."

"You'd be surprised how much pride the remaining inhabitants *do* take in their village. The ones that stayed behind after the mine failed and their descendants are almost fiercely proud of Tregeagle, odd as that might seem."

Ida paused whatever she was doing by the sink. "I'm not sure that pride is the right word," she said. "It's more that they are protective of the village. Possessive even."

Arthur nodded. "Yes, you may be right, love. Never say a bad word about Tregeagle to any of the locals. I don't include your aunt in that term, by the way. I mean the villagers who have spent all their lives there."

Something Arthur had said, almost in passing, nagged at me. "Arthur," I began. "What did you mean when you said that some of the villagers were driven out?"

"My father had some strange tales to tell about those times. Rumours abounded of queer goings-on. Dad would often go into the village for a few jars in the *Smugglers*. He said that some of the stories he heard must have been inspired by too much ale. Others, he wasn't so sure."

I sat forward. "What sort of stories?"

"Well, the mine, even before it was played out, was supposed to be haunted."

"Where is the mine?"

"In the woods—more a forest these days—above the village."

"Oh, I've been quite a way into that forest and saw no sign of a mine."

"You could walk right over it and not know it was there. They filled it in."

"Why?"

"There was a tragedy connected with it. Apparently, not long after it had given up the last of its tin ore, a man and his wife stepped into the shaft in a suicide pact. My father never told me the couple's names and I've never been able to find out from the villagers. They refuse to talk about it."

"That's why it was filled in, because that couple killed themselves?"

"It was worse than that." He glanced up at his wife who shook her head. "It's all right Ida. He's old enough to hear the whole story." He looked at me. "It was worse than just a crazy man and his wife doing away with themselves. You see, they had two children, a boy and a girl. Barely more than toddlers according to my father's account. The man and his wife each held a child in their arms as they stepped off the edge."

I shuddered and took a larger sip of cider.

Arthur went on: "So they backfilled the shaft and people started to drift away from the village. Other peculiar things were supposed to have happened. Animals went berserk for no apparent reason. Ghostly apparitions were glimpsed in the forest and within the village. A few previously sane men and women claimed to be possessed by evil spirits. A strange blue glow was witnessed. My father said that he saw the blue light once. It was coming from the mine shaft before it was filled in."

I swallowed hard. Arthur fixed me with a piercing gaze.

"Have *you* noticed anything odd about the village?" he asked.

I tried to keep my tone conversational. "Well, yes I have as a matter of fact."

He raised his eyebrows in enquiry. I did not want to tell him about the Dead Lights, the Meadow or my encounter in bed with the girl thing. I did not know him well enough and was afraid to put him off telling me more by making him think he had a madman in his kitchen.

Instead I said, "For a start the villagers are very unfriendly, at least those I've met. Most of them stay indoors or in their back gardens. There's never anybody on the green or in the pub as far as I've noticed."

Arthur nodded. "I don't go to the village much these days. Sometimes I deliver to the shop but mostly John and Kevin—he's my other son-in-law—do the shop run. I do however pass through every couple of weeks on my way to market. The village is always deserted."

We were both silent for a moment. Then Arthur said, "Anything else you've noticed?"

I took another mouthful of cider before answering. "Aye," I said, "the birds. They don't sing in the village." I looked at him anxiously, afraid he'd laugh. When his expression remained grave, I carried on speaking in a rush. "It's really weird. Go out of the village a couple of hundred yards and they start to sing and call quite normally. Inside the village they don't make a sound. I thought it was supposed to be like that when I first came here, me being a city boy and all that. It's not normal though is it?"

"No," said Arthur. "It most certainly is not."

I felt my shoulders sag with relief at hearing it confirmed.

Ida had turned and was listening intently to our conversation. "Tell John about Shep and Sheba, love," she said.

"They're our dogs," said Arthur.

"Me and Shep have met," I said, indicating the still damp patch on my shirt.

Arthur chuckled. "A slobbery mutt is our Shep. So how many dogs, or cats come to that, have you seen in the village?"

I thought about it. "Hmm . . . I don't recall seeing any."

"That's because there aren't any dogs or cats there at all to my knowledge. The only animals in Tregeagle are pigs, poultry, sheep and such like and most of them are penned in. Country folk are fond of domesticated animals as well as wild ones. It is highly unusual that nobody at all in the village keeps a pet."

Ida spoke again. "Tell him about our dogs."

"Yes, our dogs. . . ." said Arthur. "Well, they will not go anywhere near the village. I've tried walking them, carrying them on the cart and dragging them. As soon as they reach the edge of the village their hackles rise, they start to whimper or growl and they simply refuse to go any further. If we're in the cart, they jump off and run home. Once I tied Sheba inside the cart so she couldn't run away. No sooner had we entered the village than she went absolutely frantic. Howling, snarling, biting at her tether and at me, squirting urine in all directions. I turned around and drove the cart out of the village as fast as the horse would go. I've not attempted to take either dog back since."

"But your horse will go through the village?"

"Yes, she will. She tends to lay her ears flat and speed up until we're out the other side but we've had no real problem with her. Perhaps she's not as sensitive as the dogs."

"Not as sensitive to *what*?" The back of my neck felt cold, though I was facing the breeze that came though the door.

Arthur sighed. "We don't know." His wife shrugged in agreement. "But I wonder sometimes . . . you know, even the name of the village. Tregeagle. It's an old Cornish word for demon."

"Demon. Hmm . . . What about—" I hesitated, wondering whether I really wanted to know the answer to my next questions, then plunged on. "What about Jez Kellock? Is it true what happened to him? That he killed himself with a sharpened stick?"

Arthur and Ida exchanged a glance. Ida shrugged once more.

"Yes," said Arthur. "It's true. I was a young man when it happened and I wasn't there to see what he did to himself. But I saw the body and the pool of blood on the green."

"And he'd been wandering for days in the forest, where the mine is?"

"That's what everyone thinks, though of course we can't be sure. There's no telling what drove Jez mad. Only one thing's certain and that is he *was* mad. Stark, raving mad. Only a madman could have done what he did to himself." Arthur shuddered and stared into the distance, his eyes dull.

I broke the brief silence. "I wanted to ask you about a story that you started to tell Auntie Gwen. Something about a family that lived in Tregeagle."

Arthur's brow creased as he thought. "When did I tell your aunt this story?"

"I don't know when exactly. She said that you were on the way to market and Frank Fletcher interrupted you."

"Oh yes, I remember. That charming man Frank Fletcher." He snorted. "Not a pleasant man at all is Mr Fletcher. Fortunately his daughter has not turned out to be like him. Have you met Mary?"

I nodded.

"Attractive lass is Mary, don't you think?" The twinkle reappeared in his eyes.

I shrugged non-committally. He and Ida glanced at each other and grinned. They reminded me of Ma and Gwen. I hurried on before the spreading blush could take hold.

"Please would you tell me the story you were trying to tell Auntie Gwen that day."

"There's not a lot to tell, lad," said Arthur. "A family lived in Black Tops before your aunt came to Tregeagle. The family was Irish. A father, mother and three children. This would have been about thirty years ago or more. I remember them fairly well, though I didn't really know them. Flynn I think their surname was."

"How old were the children?"

"Let's see . . . the youngest was a babe in arms. The middle one was a boy around four years old. The eldest, a girl, was about nine."

"Did she have brown hair?"

"Yes, I believe so—How did you know that?" His gaze was keen once more.

"Oh, just something that my auntie mentioned," I lied. "What happened to the family?"

"Nobody really knows what happened to them. One day, they simply disappeared. All five of them vanished into thin air. The father had been out here to ask my father for work only the day before. Dark haired, handsome fellow he was, softly spoken but very polite. My father offered him some labouring, not really needing the help but knowing that the man had three bairns to feed. He invited Mr Flynn back the next day to make a start.

"Well, Mr Flynn didn't arrive for work. As I had to run an errand to the village for my mother, my father asked me to call at Black Tops to see if Mr Flynn had changed his mind. I knocked at the front door until my knuckles ached but there was no reply. I walked round to the back of the house. The back door stood open. It was gashed and scarred as though it had been kicked repeatedly. But that was the only sign of violence I could see. I went into the kitchen and shouted but the house was empty."

Ida hadn't resumed her housework. She stood behind an empty chair listening to us, her eyes darting from me to her husband. "Tell him about the kitchen table," she murmured.

"Oh yes," said Arthur. "The kitchen table was laid and three chairs had been pushed back as if the family had been interrupted in the middle of supper. It was spooky standing there in that silent house looking at a half-eaten meal. I kept expecting the children to leap out of hiding with squeals of laughter. But they didn't. They and their parents were gone. The house was quite empty."

"Doesn't anybody know where they went?"

"Absolutely none. Or if anyone does know, they haven't shared their knowledge with me. Anyway, I ran home and told Dad what I'd found. He went to see for himself. He could find no clue to what had happened. He asked around the village but no-one could shed any light on the family's disappearance. I think my father suspected that at least some of the villagers were lying but he had nothing firm to base it on, no evidence of any wrongdoing. If he'd uncovered any evidence at all, he would have taken it to the town's constabulary."

"So what happened?"

"Nothing. We never saw or heard of the Flynn family again. The story that went round the village afterwards and eventually became accepted was that the family had simply upped and left in the middle of the night. Returned to Ireland." He snorted in derision.

"You don't believe that?"

"No. I saw the house. All their belongings were still there, everything, including the baby's things. Tell me, what kind of family leaves their home at the dead of night, in the middle of nowhere, and takes no clothes or food for their children, not even the baby's blanket or comforter? It just doesn't make sense. Still," he sighed, "it was a very long time ago."

As I pondered his words, I noticed the face of the tall grandfather clock that ticked sombrely in a corner. I stood in a rush.

"Crikey, look at the time! I've kept you talking half the afternoon. I told Auntie Gwen I'd be back around lunchtime. She was baking fresh bread to have with the butter." I held my hand out to Arthur. "Thank you very much for your hospitality. And you, Ida. I hope I haven't outstayed my welcome."

"Not at all, John," said Arthur, shaking my hand. "I've enjoyed our chat. Quite splendid. Come and see us again any time you feel like."

"Yes," echoed his wife. "It's been lovely having you. I just hope that all those stories won't give you nightmares."

As I took my leave of the couple and hurried to retrieve the butter from the dairy, I had to keep in check a strong desire to cackle hysterically.

Love

I guess that more poems and songs have been written about love than about any other topic. It pervades every art form: literature, painting, opera, film, popular music . . . the list is probably endless. Without the capacity to love we would be shallow creatures, grasping and selfish, lonely and afraid. Ideals such as honour, chivalry and loyalty stem from love. It counterbalances mankind's tendency to hate others for no better reason than they have different coloured skins or worship a different god. It tempers our greed and our envy.

The day following my visit to the Baileys is a day that is indelibly etched upon my memory. It was the day that Mary and I became lovers.

I met her in the Glade as usual. She was a vision of beauty in a plain white smock that hugged her curves.

The breeze that had made my hike to and from the farm bearable had dropped to the merest whisper that made the leaves shiver but did little to cool the fever that surged through me at the sight of Mary.

She stood in the shade with her back to the trunk of a tree. I strode towards her.

With all that had happened recently, I felt different that day. It was as though some watershed had been reached. Things were moving quickly and a climax was approaching like a runaway train that I was powerless to halt. I did not want to waste any time.

Mary's welcoming smile turned to a frown as she took in my serious expression and my purposeful stride.

"John . . . what's wrong?"

I did not speak. Acting like a man possessed, I placed the palms of my hands to her cheeks and kissed her full on the lips. Her hands came up to grip my wrists but she made no attempt to pull away. Her lips tasted even sweeter without a coating of salt.

Reluctantly I pulled back but my hands continued to cup her face, preventing her from looking away. She was breathing heavily and her eyes sparkled like black diamonds in the sunlight. I stared deep into their depths.

"I love you Mary. I've loved you since the moment I first saw you. I love you more than I thought I could ever love anyone." There. It was out.

During my earlier teenage years, I had often fantasised about what it would be like to one day say those words to a girl. Toe-curlingly embarrassing was my best guess. I could not have been more wrong. I felt no flush of self-consciousness, no urge to drop my gaze and shuffle my feet. The overwhelming emotion that swept over me was one of huge relief. It mattered not that she may not have felt the same way about me; that her reaction might have been to laugh or, worse, to pity me.

She stared back at me. As the feeling of relief receded, a worm of doubt started to grow. But Mary threw her arms around my neck and showered my lips with frantic kisses. I kissed her madly back and started to laugh. I could not help it. I felt delirious, drunk upon the potency of what I felt for her.

We both laughed, roaring and rolling as if we would never have the opportunity to experience happiness ever again. An onlooker would have assumed we were quite mad. Perhaps during those few minutes we were.

At last the hysterics subsided and we stood just looking at each other. Now it was Mary's turn to wear a serious expression. As she gazed intently into my face, her lips came apart and she moistened them with her tongue. Her chest heaved, breasts straining against the white cotton material. Her eyes grew wider and darker.

My own breath came heavily. I was vaguely conscious of my heart thudding in my chest and acutely aware of an almost painful throbbing lower down.

Mary took me by the hand. "Come on," she breathed.

I nodded. I doubt that I could have spoken even had I tried. I followed obediently as she led me out of the Glade. Kicking off her shoes and discarding them in the grass, she paddled across the stream. Not wanting to break the connection by letting go of her hand to take off my boots, I left them on and splashed through the brook immediately behind her. I had no idea where she was leading me. Neither was I paying much notice. My attention was too fixed upon the way her body moved beneath her dress.

When we stopped, we were in the middle of a thick stand of trees that circled and sheltered us from any prying eyes. Grass, sprinkled liberally with sun-yellow buttercups, grew abundantly in the patch of sunlight that penetrated the circle. These things I noticed later. For now, I only had eyes for her.

She released my hand and faced me. Neither of us speaking, she reached behind her and slowly unbuttoned her dress. Her gaze never leaving mine, she pulled the material free and let it slip to the ground. She wore nothing beneath the dress.

Then she was in my arms.

We lay on the soft bed of grass and gave ourselves to each other. It passed in a daze of sweet, sweet ecstasy. Looking back now and even in the days immediately afterwards, I cannot and could not recall clearly those moments of the first fulfilment of our passion. They are blanketed in a haze of mixed emotions—unbridled pleasure and joy, astonishment at my good fortune and, overriding all else, deep and pure love. It is the only blip on my memory.

Afterwards we lay side by side, our skins dappled by sunlight that broke through the canopy of leaves. My whole body tingled with the afterglow of lovemaking. Mary's cheeks were bright with colour. Her hand played absent-mindedly with the medallion around my neck.

Then I noticed a tear roll down one cheek. I brushed it away with my fingers.

"What's the matter?"

She looked at me with eyes that sparkled like freshly polished crystal. "Nothing's the matter. I'm just incredibly happy."

"Do you always cry when you're happy?"

"Course not. It's just that. . . ." She heaved a big sigh. "Look, John. I love you too. We're meant to be together. I felt it the first time I saw you standing by the water pump trying to figure out how it worked."

My heart, already engorged by the depth of my feelings, threatened to burst at her words. I cupped her chin in my hand and held her gaze. "I'm the happiest person alive when I'm with you. I want you to be happy when you're with me."

"I *am* happy. I never want us to be apart. But. . . ."

"But what?"

She pulled away from my hand. Wiping the last of her tears away, she said, "But nothing. It doesn't matter. I'm going back to the stream."

"What for?"

"To clean myself up. I won't be long."

"But—you're not dirty."

"Men!" She raised her eyes to the heavens. "That was my first time. I'm bleeding from . . . well, down below."

"Oh. It was my first time too."

She grinned. "I know. I could tell."

"Could you? *Really?*"

"No, silly. I'm teasing."

She shrugged into her dress. The sight transfixed me. She smiled impishly and jiggled her breasts as they disappeared from my eager view. Then she knelt and kissed me, a firm lingering kiss.

Mary was breathing heavily again. She spoke and her voice was husky. "That may have been our first time but it better not have been the last!"

She rose and left the tiny clearing, forcing her way past branches and leaves. We must have pushed through them to enter the circle of trees but I had been oblivious to my surroundings at the time, conscious only of the girl holding my hand.

I lay on my back and stared at the blue circle above the tops of the trees. I felt contented, at ease with the world. But it did not last long. Do good times ever? Dark thoughts started to intrude upon my pleasant musings and I went over in my mind the events of two nights previously when my sleep had been disturbed by the creature with weed in its hair. The memory made me shiver despite the warmth of the afternoon.

Then I mentally replayed the lengthy conversation I'd had the previous day with Mr and Mrs Bailey—or Arthur and Ida as I was quick to correct myself. I had hoped there would be some rational explanation for the birds shunning the village, but there was apparently not one. Worse, it was not confined to our feathered friends. Dogs and cats shied away from the village too, at least according to Arthur and his wife. I did not doubt their word for a second. I had not seen a single dog or cat in Tregeagle and I had now lived there for nigh on four months.

I was pondering upon what might have happened to the Flynn family who once inhabited Black Tops when the branches in front of me started to rustle and Mary pushed back into the clearing. All signs of her tears had been washed away. She looked fresh-faced and vital. My expression must have been sombre for she frowned as she sat down beside me.

"What are you thinking about? Nothing particularly pleasant if the look on your face is anything to go by."

I wondered what, if anything, I should tell her. There was clearly something happening out of the ordinary. It clearly had something to do with me. But what if by telling Mary about it I somehow dragged her into it? I certainly did not want her to become involved. Yet, I sensed that somehow she was already involved, that every inhabitant of Tregeagle was somehow embroiled in whatever was going on. So I decided to tell Mary what had happened to me since I had come to her village. I would take the risk that she might think I needed to be locked away in a lunatic asylum.

First, though, I slipped into my clothes. Unlikely though it was to happen, especially hidden away in the thicket as we were, I did not want somebody from the village to blunder across us with me stark naked except for the St Christopher. God forbid that it should be Ma or Gwen out on one of their rambles. But more than that, my dark thoughts made me feel vulnerable and I would be a lot more comfortable relaying them to Mary with my clothes on.

Once dressed, I sat down beside Mary and talked. I told her about my meetings with Callum in the Meadow and how I was convinced that they were more than simple dreams. I told her of the strange man's voice that I had heard coming from Gwen's bedroom and how I had burst in only to find my aunt alone and asleep. I related my encounter with Mitch Mahoney. I told her about the Dead Lights that seemed to shine from the pond. Haltingly, I narrated my experience with the girl-thing in my bed. Finally, I repeated as closely word-for-word as I could the things that Arthur and Ida Bailey had told me. The only part I deliberately omitted was the reference to her father's unpleasant character.

As I spoke, a variety of emotions played across her face. I was relieved that disbelief was not one of them. A look of wonder came into her eyes as I talked about the Meadow. At times she looked concerned—she gripped my hand tightly as I told her of the fight with Mitch. At other times she appeared shocked. By the time I had finished talking, she looked terrified.

She grabbed both my hands in hers and spoke urgently. "You asked me earlier why I was upset. It was because I don't want to lose you so soon after I've found you. I can sense something is wrong too. Something about the village. I don't know why and I can't explain quite what I feel, but I don't think we have much of a future together." She put a finger to my lips before grasping my hand again. "Shh! Let me finish. I feel . . . no, I *know* deep down that we haven't got long together. There's an awful sense of doom hanging over me. The feeling has always been there, I see that now. Meeting you has brought it to the surface. One of us, or both of us more likely, are in some sort of danger . . . something connected with Tregeagle. Oh, John, I'm afraid."

I held her in my arms. She was shivering. "Hey, it's all right. Whatever is going on here, I don't think it can hurt us." I spoke the words with such certainty that I almost believed them myself.

Mary pulled away from my embrace and spoke with even more urgency. "Why don't we get away from here? Pack a bag and just walk away. You could take me to Newcastle or we could go to Wales. I want us to grow old together and that ain't going to happen if we stay here!" She spoke the last sentence fiercely, her accent thickened by emotion.

I reckon that barely a single day has gone by in the ensuing years when I have not thought back to that moment and wished with all my might that I had agreed to Mary's request. We could have done it—simply packed a few clothes and some food and walked out of Tregeagle for ever. I could have left Ma a note explaining that I had gone to Wales and would look up some of her relatives. She would have worried, sure, but she was sufficiently recovered for it not to have knocked her back too much. Neither Mary nor I had any money but the community spirit of the war would still have been evident, I'm sure, at least outside Tregeagle. People would have helped us. Besides, we were young and fit. We could have worked our way to Wales with little difficulty.

But at that moment I could not foresee what was going to happen. Had I known, I would not have even stopped to pack a bag.

I shook my head. "I can't leave. Ma is only just getting used to the idea of losing her husband, her eldest son and her only daughter. I can't desert her now."

Mary sighed in resignation. "Yeah, I know. No matter. It was just a thought."

"We'll work something out, don't worry." I sounded more confident than I felt.

"Yeah, I'm sure we will." She said it without conviction.

As we headed back to the village in the early evening, I felt as though I had let her down.

But we walked with our arms entwined and she kissed me long and hard as we parted. With the promise of seeing her again in two days' time ringing in my ears, I headed for Black Tops.

Ma and Gwen had taken kitchen chairs into the back garden and were enjoying the relative coolness of the evening as the sun started its slow descent below the horizon. I took out a chair and joined them, gladly accepting the proffered glass of watered wine. I was still pretty much on a high—after all, it's not every day that you lose your virginity—and had barely noticed quite how parched my throat had become.

Gwen cleared her throat and I could see from the corner of my eye her nudging Ma. "You look like the cat who's got the cream, Johnny Boy. Had a good day?"

"Aye, that I have, Auntie Gwen," I replied equably. She could tease me all she wanted that evening.

"Where you been then, *cariad?*"

"Oh, you know, here and there."

"On your own was it?"

"Well, no, actually. I've been out with Mary." For once, I did not blush upon mentioning her name.

"So, are you two courting now?"

"Um . . . do you know, I suppose that we are. Yes, Mary and I are courting." It felt good to say it.

Ma and Gwen both looked pleased at the news. And my frank admission had taken the wind out of my aunt's sails. The teasing stopped before it had barely begun.

"You'll have to bring her round to meet me, John," said Ma.

"I will. You'll really like her, Ma."

"You will at that," agreed Gwen. "She's a lovely girl. Very unlike her father, thank goodness. There's no prettier girl around than that one. They'll make handsome grandchildren for you."

Now the blush did start. I arose and strolled down the garden, pausing to scratch Banger's ears as I passed.

I reached the garden's end and leaned against the wall, my arms resting upon the stile. I gazed out across the field.

There is something about the light at a certain moment on a summer's evening when it has been cloudless and hot all day. It has a pure quality that is unsullied by glare or haze of daytime heat. Maybe it is only the novelty of being able to look in every direction without having to shield your eyes from the sun, but I always gain the impression on such evenings that I can see much further than should normally be humanly possible.

As I relaxed against the stile, that optimum moment had arrived. The sun had that instant disappeared from the sky and it would be dark very soon. For now though it was still quite light and the air had that perfect quality that always makes me want to gaze my fill of my surroundings in almost reverential wonder.

But not that evening. My gaze was drawn time after time to just one spot. The pond.

I suppose that the muddy water hole had grown in significance in my mind since the advent of the Dead Lights. They did after all appear to originate from the pond or from somewhere very near to it.

But that was not why my eyes kept returning to it that evening, though I cannot put my finger upon the exact reason.

All I can say is that I suddenly felt inexplicably cold as I looked at that pond. A strong sense of foreboding crept up my spine and the hairs on my arms and neck prickled as though I had received a mild electric shock.

Some part of me knew that whatever was going on, the pond had something to do with it. That same part of me knew that I had some business with that pond, and it would not be pleasant. No, not pleasant at all.

Smuggler's Reach

During that long hot summer of 1947, I understood that many of the occurrences I was experiencing were not born of the natural world. I knew, of course, that I was dealing with the supernatural. Yet I suspected that the root causes lay in the everyday world and determined to try to ascertain what those causes were. I reckoned that I might stand a better chance of combating the supernatural forces that were at work if I understood what was driving them.

The only plan that suggested itself was to persuade one of the villagers to talk. The major flaw was that the village was inhabited by a bunch of hermits who seemed even less likely to want to talk to me than to each other.

Mary aside, there was only one villager I'd met who hadn't displayed any hostility, though I was not in the least encouraged that he would be able to tell me anything useful. On the other hand, he may have overheard others talking about the village's past. After all, he worked in a place where gossip and rumour were rife. Furthermore, I reasoned, it was approaching lunchtime on yet another breathless summer's day. There was bound to be a villager or two enjoying a refreshing lunchtime pint of ale whom maybe I could engage in conversation.

Morning chores done, I headed for the tavern.

Passing the green, the water pump standing forlornly like a forgotten sentinel, I arrived at *The Smugglers' Reach* without seeing another person. The same gloom and silence met me when I opened the door as on the previous occasion I'd entered the public bar. Yet the interior had the familiar smell of a bar: yeast, hops and stale tobacco smoke. Even though currently deserted, the tavern must have received custom recently.

I walked up to the wooden expanse of the bar and called, "Hello!"

As I waited for a response, I leaned against the bar and let my gaze wander idly over the empty tables, stools and benches. A glint caught my eye from beneath the table next to the door. I strolled over and stooped. A penny lay on the floor. I returned to the bar with it tightly in my grasp.

I called again, louder. There came the shuffling sound of footsteps and the man who had pointed us to Black Tops on our arrival appeared from the door behind the bar. He was as huge as I remembered and his round face was again slack and vacant. His greasy hair had been cut short, by a blunt knife judging by the scraggy look of it.

He shambled his massive bulk to a halt and turned to face me. His florid skin glistened with perspiration although it was markedly cooler inside the tavern than outside. His head resembled a vast sweating cheese, an image reinforced by the ripe odour that washed over me like an invalid's breath.

I forced a smile, which is easier said than done while struggling not to breathe through your nose. "Hello," I said. "We've met before. I'm John, Gwen Evans's nephew."

I waited for my words to register.

He merely stood and stared at me, expressionless.

"Um," I said. "I'll have a pint of your best bitter please."

This must have been a request with which he was familiar for he bent wordlessly and retrieved a tankard from beneath the bar. He shuffled his huge frame along to the beer pump and pulled a pint. The ale gurgled as it frothed into the tankard and I licked my lips in anticipation. He placed the brimming pot of beer on the bar before me, surprisingly gently for such a giant. He held out one huge hand expectantly.

"Thank you," I said. "How much?"

He cleared his throat. It sounded like the growl of an angry bear. "Ha'penny." I was once more struck by how incongruously soft his voice was.

I handed over the penny. "Hang on to the change," I said. "I'll be having another in a minute."

The next few moments were lost in the pleasure of supping cool bitter on a hot summer's day. I sank half the contents of the tankard in one deep draught and slapped my lips in contentment, luxuriating in the aftertaste of hops and barley. As I raised the tankard to drain it, I realised that the man was still standing in front of me, hand out flat with the penny resting on the palm.

I drained the tankard and held it out. "Same again please. You keep a fine drop of bitter in your kegs."

At these words, the man's features at last became animated. A faint smile slowly seeped into his face and his eyes became alert.

"Aye," he said. "You'll not find a better beer in these parts."

He plodded laboriously the few steps to the pump and refilled the tankard. I felt it would be churlish to point out that his was the *only* beer to be found in these parts, at least within a ten mile radius, so I kept my mouth shut. I didn't want to risk putting him in a bad mood now that he had become so chatty.

He placed the full tankard before me almost tenderly. Conscious that I was once more bereft of the king's coin, I resisted the urge to gulp this one.

"Your good health," I said as I raised the tankard and took a sip. "What's your name?"

It took a moment during which I imagined I could hear his inner circuitry making the necessary connections. Then he answered: "Martin."

"Have you lived here all your life, Martin?"

Another pause. "Aye. That I have."

"Do you like living in Tregeagle?"

A frown gathered upon his broad brow, like thunderheads clustering around a mountaintop. After what seemed an age, he replied: "No. But Da lives here."

"What about your ma?" No sooner was the question out that I remembered that Gwen had told me she had been friendly with the innkeeper's wife—presumably Martin's mother—and that she had died. I silently cursed myself for my stupidity.

Martin's frown deepened. "She went to the angels."

I moved on quickly. "I went to see Arthur Bailey the other day. Do you know Arthur out at the farm?"

I was relieved to see his dark expression lift. He nodded. "Aye. He's got dogs. Woof! Woof!" He made a strange choking sound deep in his throat that alarmed me until I realised that he was laughing. I joined in.

"Have you been out to the farm to see his dogs?" I asked. "Arthur told me that Shep and Sheba won't come into the village."

"Nah. They're scairt."

"Scairt? Oh—what are they afraid of Martin?"

"Can't tell. Da says I mustn't talk to outsiders."

"But I'm not an outsider," I said. "I live here in the village . . . at Black Tops. You know, with my Auntie Gwen. Miss Evans."

Martin smiled again. "Aye. I knows Miss Evans. She be from Wales."

"That's right. Did you know the people who lived in Miss Evans's house before she came here?"

He shook his head.

"The farmer told me that their name was Flynn," I said. "They were from Ireland."

He said nothing but I thought I saw a faint light of recognition glimmer in his eyes. I took a sip of beer while I pondered how to proceed.

"They had three children," I said. "One of them a baby. Mr Bailey told me that one night they just disappeared. Isn't that strange?"

"Drownded."

"Pardon?"

"Drownded," repeated Martin. "The babba an' all."

"What? They drowned? The whole family?"

"Aye."

"But how . . . where? Did you see it happen?"

He shook his head ponderously, like a great bear.

I took another long sip of beer. "Martin," I said. "Somebody round here must know what happened to them. You must have heard someone talking about it. Have you?"

He sighed and bowed his head. Another waft of sour breath washed over me, but I didn't look away. I watched as Martin raised his head and could not help but shudder at the changed expression on his face.

Gone was the face of a gentle simpleton. It had been replaced by an expression of animal cunning. His eyes narrowed and darted from side to side like the eyes of a trapped rat. When he spoke, an icy tendril licked up my back.

"Held 'em under. Dirty Irish fuckers. Got what they deserved. Let 'em scream, let 'em kick, let 'em drink 'til they burst." The incongruously soft voice had gone too. The words were spoken in a gruff tone, harsh and menacing.

"Martin?" I asked tentatively. The gentle giant had been replaced by somebody with far more intelligence and a lot more meanness.

He opened his mouth and the same harsh voice spoke again. "Up and down, bib and bob. The bairns was easy. But it took three of us to hold him. And the fucking bitch . . . hee hee, scrammed and bit like a badger in a trap. A fucking Irish bitch in a trap. Stood on her head. That kept her down. Bitch ate mud."

I held my breath, my drink forgotten. Martin spoke again.

"We showed 'em. Fucking potato-picking interlopers." He laughed. Low and coarse, filled with spite.

"Martin?" I said again. "Are you all right?"

A shiver ran through him, like a tree rustling in a sudden breeze. He looked at me and his expression was his own again: a little vacant, a little simple, but with no hint of malice.

"Aye," he said in his own gentle voice. "I be fine. Why shouldn't I be?"

"You sounded, um, different. Like you were someone else."

He shrugged. "You asked if I heard anything. I tell you."

I remembered my drink and picked up the tankard.

The term *idiot savant* was not one I was familiar with at the time. It is no longer considered a politically correct term to describe someone like Martin, but I am certain that is what he was. He had just repeated to me, I suspect word-for-word, a speech he had heard probably many years previously, in the same tone of voice and expression of the original speaker.

"When did you hear those words, Martin?" I asked.

He thought for a moment. "When I was a bairn."

"A long time ago?"

Shrug.

"Who said those things?" I asked.

Martin's brow knitted into another frown. "Man. Bad man."

"A man from the village?"

Nod.

"Do you know his name?" I was holding my breath again, afraid to press too hard yet feeling almost desperate to learn the identity of the original speaker.

"Aye." Martin's voice dropped to little more than a whisper and I had to strain to hear him.

"Will you tell me his name, Martin? Please?"

"Da tole me never to tell." His hands had come together and he was wringing them like a young child being told off.

"I won't tell your Da that you told me." I glanced around at the empty bar and lowered my voice to a mock conspiratorial whisper. "It'll be our secret."

As the cogs turned, a smile resurfaced on his face and he nodded.

"Aye. A secret. Our secret. Yahoo!"

"Shh! Secrets have to be told quietly. Otherwise they aren't secrets any more."

He nodded soberly.

"So . . . ?" I said. "Martin, you can tell me his name now."

"Huh?"

"The man who said those things. The bad man. What was his name?" I struggled to keep the impatience out of my voice. "Martin?"

He leaned towards me across the smooth wooden surface of the bar. Again my nostrils were assailed by the sour-milk odour of his breath, but I fought the urge to turn away. In a stage whisper, he spoke a name. "Frank Fletcher."

I gasped. "Are you sure?"

"Aye," he said, straightening. "I heard him."

"Could it have been someone who looked like him or sounded like him? Are you positive it *was* him?"

"It was him. I saw him. I remember."

Just then another voice spoke, loudly. "Martin! What are you doing?"

A man entered the bar through the same door from which Martin had emerged. He was old and grizzled, bent over a cane that clunked on the wooden floor as he hobbled forward. The facial features were similar to Martin's, but without the slack, vacant expression that Martin's face habitually wore. At that moment, the old man's face wore a deep scowl that creased the aged skin that covered his skull like the husk of a shrivelled conker.

"Who are you talking to?" the old man spat. "Imbecile!" He hobbled forward to the bar so that he could get a better look at me. His eyes narrowed in a look of deep mistrust. "Who are you?"

I cleared my throat. "John Andrews, sir. I live at Black Tops with my aunt and my mother." I raised the tankard and sipped at what remained of my beer.

"If you're twenty-one then I'm the King of England." He shifted his attention back to Martin who stood still, head lowered. "Don't just stand there, moron. Fetch my dinner." He raised the cane as if to strike Martin who recoiled in fear. Had he the wit, Martin could have broken the old man like a dry twig. Instead he muttered something that I didn't catch and lumbered out of the rear door. The old man grimaced. "Idiot! Should have drowned him at birth."

He seemed to have momentarily forgotten my presence. I used the brief respite to drain the tankard. As I plonked it empty onto the bar, he shifted his fierce gaze in my direction once more. "You still here?" he growled.

"Uh, just on my way." I started to back away from the bar.

His expression darkened further and his eyes narrowed to slits. "What were you talking to my idiot son about, eh?"

"Nothing," I muttered. "Just passing the time of day."

"Sounded like you were being a nosy little bastard to me."

I bit my tongue, choking back the retort. I felt sorry for Martin and had no desire to make his situation worse by riling the old man. "It was nothing but idle chatter."

He snorted. "Idle chatter! That boy wouldn't know idle chatter if it bit him on the arse. Look, boy. This here public house is for men, not kids. Least of all foreign little twerps like you. Stay away from here if you know what's good for you."

Foreign! It took all my willpower not to tell the old man precisely what I thought of him. I managed to get out through gritted teeth, "Aye, I will."

"Good. It'll save me breaking my stick over your backside. I'll have to break it over my son's thick head instead."

He cackled and the sound followed me as I backed through the tavern door and out into the sunshine.

Village of Lost Souls

Black Tops was deserted when I arrived back from the tavern. Ma and Gwen were out on one of their afternoon rambles. I took a chair into the back garden and settled down in a patch of shade to ponder what I had learned from Martin.

The air was warm and still. Apart from the buzzing of the odd passing bee and the occasional soft cluck or grunt, it was very peaceful in the garden. The two pints I had supped at the inn had been enough to make me drowsy.

My eyelids grew too heavy to hold up and I quickly passed into an easy slumber . . .

. . . and found myself back in the Meadow.

It was sunny there too. I rose to my knees and looked around for Callum. He was standing behind me. I jumped to my feet and hugged him.

Callum returned the hug. As I pulled away, I could see his expression was serious, verging on grim.

"Cal, are you all right?" I asked.

"As fine as can be in the circumstances," he replied. "You?"

"Okay, I suppose."

"And Ma?"

"Oh, she's well now, Cal. It's done her the world of good coming to Cornwall. She and Auntie Gwen have sort of healed each other."

"Gwen . . . I remember. Ma's sister." A sad look passed across his face. "Has anything strange been happening to you, John?"

"Aye. You could say that. What do you know about these things?"

"I know a little but not enough. You've met Mitch here."

"Yes. How did you know?"

"We've sort of bumped into each other in the other place . . . Darkland. He bragged about how he'd beaten you up and how you begged him to stop. I knew he was lying."

"Well, it was touch and go for a little while but I escaped from him easily in the end. He can't hurt me any more. But you . . . ?"

My brother smiled grimly. "Oh yes. He can still hurt me, if I let him that is. Mitch and I have unfinished business. We'll be attending to it presently."

"Cal, be careful. He's an animal. Can't you just keep away from him?" Even as I spoke the words I knew that Callum would never run away from a fight. Not even now that he inhabited some place between places.

"Don't think I can do that even if I wanted to. Mitch is part of the reason I've not yet passed on. I still don't understand it fully but I know that I must fight him again before I can leave Darkland."

"There must be a way—"

"No. I have to face him again. Then I can leave."

"Is it a terrible place?"

"It's pretty bloody grim. There's not many of my sort there."

"Your sort?"

Callum thought for a moment. "Has Ma ever told you her theory about there being no pure good or evil?"

I remembered that conversation with Ma at the height of the war. "Aye," I said. "No black or white. Just shades of grey."

"That's the one. Well she was right up to a point. There *are* absolute forces . . . black and white, good and evil, God and the Devil, call them what you will. But nobody in your world contains just one of those absolutes. Living people are made up of a mixture of opposing forces. In some, white is in the ascendancy; in others, black is the dominant force. That's a little simplistic but it'll do."

"Like Hitler," I said. "There wasn't much white in him."

"Hitler . . . yes. I forget so easily. You said 'wasn't'—is he dead?"

I nodded. "Took the coward's way out. Shot himself before the Russians could string him up."

Callum's brow creased in puzzlement. "The Russians? They fought *against* Germany?"

"Yep. Probably Hitler's biggest mistake attacking them. I take it Hitler's not with you in Darkland then?"

"Nope. Don't recall him passing through either, unless. . . ."

"Unless what?"

"There was a time. . . ." Callum frowned as if 'time' was not the correct word but he couldn't think of another. "There was a time when all became still. The little light that's in Darkland faded entirely away so that there weren't even shadows. I felt a great surge pass by me, like some terrible wind blown straight from Hell itself. I was afraid and threw myself to the ground. All at once I was surrounded by a dreadful noise. It sounded like the wailing of thousands or millions of souls in the depths of torment. Their anguish and distress was truly horrifying and heart-wrenching to hear. The wailing followed in the wake of the wind and was gone. Only when all was silent once more did the shadows return. I welcomed them. Anything was better than that awful chorus of despair." He shuddered.

"Maybe that was him."

"Maybe." Callum shook his head as if to dispel the memory. "But back to what I was saying. Ma's theory is correct in the sense that no person is wholly black or white. They are all shades of grey. The inhabitants of Darkland are too but the shades are more pronounced. So Mitch now has much more darkness in him than he did when he was alive. He is still a shade of grey but a very dark shade, almost black. There are many more there like Mitch."

"What about you, Cal? Are you a lighter shade, almost white?"

Callum nodded. "It sounds too simple, too childish, but that's the way it is. There aren't many of the lighter sort in Darkland."

"Is there anybody else there you know from . . . from *before*, other than Mitch?"

"One or two but they don't concern us."

A thought struck me. "Is our grandfather there? Ma's father?"

Callum looked at me keenly. "How did you know that? Yes, he's there. I don't know why."

"I think I do. I bet he's a dark shade."

My brother nodded. "Forget about him. He's part of someone else's story."

"So what about our story? Am I still in danger? Is Ma?"

"Ma's safe. You're not." He sighed. "I have been trying to find out more but they give little away."

"Who are *they*?"

"You don't want to know and I can't tell you anyway. Let's just say that they are the guardians of Darkland and they serve the absolute powers. We inhabit the place at their bidding and cannot pass on until we complete the tasks they ordain."

"How can you carry out tasks if they won't tell you what they are?"

"I will know when the time is at hand. It will be soon. . . ." Again he frowned as though the concept of time was alien to him. "There is only one way I can help you at this meeting."

"And that is . . . ?"

"The danger that threatens you is an echo of something that took place many years ago, before even I was born."

I nodded. "I've been trying to find out what happened in Tregeagle.

It's only a small village, Cal, but a lot of strange stuff seems to have happened there over the years."

"There are places where the barrier between your world and Darkland is thin. Some who walk in Darkland can enter your world at those places if what drives them is strong enough to overcome the barrier. Since those driving forces are often hatred and a need for revenge, which are both very powerful, they can come and go almost at will. I think the village that you speak of is such a place where the barrier is stretched."

"Hmm . . . the Village of Lost Souls," I murmured, thinking back to my conversation with Gwen. "Maybe it is a good name after all."

"Well," said Callum, "they *are* lost in the sense that they cannot move on to whatever lies beyond. Trapped may be a better description."

"So, if the barrier is stretched thinly in Tregeagle . . . ?"

"In such places it is easily breached by those who had some connection to the place or the people inhabiting it. They are able to influence what happens in your world. Thus they perpetuate the cycle of events that perhaps was the cause of their deaths in the first instance."

"Not sure that I follow you, Cal."

"No matter. Just understand that the danger you face is not of your world."

"That I do understand. What will happen?"

"What will be will be. I can only show you what once was. A glimpse is permitted. Close your eyes."

I did as he asked. Immediately a mental image wavered into view, like someone else's thought inserted into my mind. The image shimmered as though I looked at a reflection in a gently undulating pool. That impression was heightened by the fact that the scene I watched was taking place in a dark expanse of water.

People stood in the water, their faces illuminated by the blue glow that shone all around them. A man was being held by three others. One had a tight grip around his neck; the other two held his arms. Nearby two men held a woman by the hair and arms. Both captives struggled in vain—they were being gripped too tightly.

A little further away a young boy, barely older than a toddler, was held by one man. The water came no higher than the lower part of the man's waist, but lapped at the child's chest. The boy was crying in terror and I was glad I could hear no sound.

Other men and a handful of women stood watching, water up to their waists. There must have been at least twenty people in total standing in the inky water, bathed in the blue glow.

A man stood in front of the captives, bending forward into the water, arms submerged to the biceps. Every head was turned towards him. To one side of the man, a bundle of rags floated just beneath the surface.

There was something vaguely familiar about this man. He was dark-haired and well-built, though gave the impression of youth. I doubted he was much older than late teens. Maybe twenty at most. I could not make out his face at first since he stared down into the depths of the lake or river or whatever it was they were standing in. The image did not extend far enough either way for me to be able to make out what the stretch of water was part of.

Then the man straightened, bringing his arms clear of the water. Something shot up in front of him, something that I recognised immediately. The face twisted in agony as it gasped for air, but there was no doubt. A frond of weed dropping down her brow, it was the young girl who had visited my bed. Water lapped at her heaving chest as she gulped in air, face contorted, eyes wide and bewildered.

As the girl's lungs filled with air, she tried to back away from the man. But he was too quick. He grabbed her by the shoulders and said something. The girl opened her mouth to scream, allowing water to rush in as the man forced her backwards beneath the surface. The man's face twisted in triumph. Still using both arms to hold the girl down, he glanced round at the other captives and I knew with sickening certainty that the girl would not surface alive again.

I had a clear view of the man's face that confirmed my suspicion that he was barely out of his teens. But that wasn't what struck me most about him. I was looking at a male version of Mary. A version that sneered and taunted and exuded malice. Despite these contrasts with Mary's guileless purity, I had no doubt that the man I was watching drown a nine-year-old girl was Frank Fletcher.

As their daughter was submerged by Fletcher, the two adult captives grew frantic in their efforts to escape. The woman nearly succeeded. One of the onlooking men waded forward and, with a vicious swing of his arm, smashed his bunched fist into the woman's face. Blood spurted from her nose and she sagged into the arms of the men holding her.

I swallowed hard and the image began to waver, then fade. Before it disappeared entirely I had time to realise that what I had taken to be a floating bundle of rags near Frank Fletcher was in fact something completely different. A swaddled baby lay face down in the water, bobbing gently in the motion caused by its sister's dying struggles.

My eyes snapped open to the sunlit vista of the Meadow. I bent forward and rested my hands on my thighs, breathing heavily. When I straightened, Callum was watching me, tenderness in his expression.

"Cal," I said, trying to keep my tone even. "That was horrible. Did that really happen?"

"Yes. A long time ago. It's connected to something that's happening now." Again that slight look of puzzlement at terms like 'time' and 'now'.

"That man—the one who was drowning the little girl . . . I know him, Cal. At least I know who he is."

"Have nothing to do with him, John. I don't need to tell you that, I hope."

I glanced down at my feet, then looked my brother in the eye. "I'm in love with his daughter."

Callum's face darkened as though a shadow had passed across it. "Stay away from her, John."

I shrugged. "I can't. Didn't you hear me? I love her. She loves me too."

"She is not my concern." He glanced briefly away as though his name had been called in a voice only he could hear. "Be careful, little brother."

I opened my mouth to say more but he was gone, winking out of sight like an extinguished flame. My stomach fluttered with the familiar pang of regret I always felt at that moment, then the Meadow was gone too.

Judging by the short distance the sun had arced across the sky, my nap had not lasted for more than an hour. It was still mid afternoon.

Although the sun continued to blaze down and it must have been in the high twenties in the shade where I sat, I shivered.

Doubting whether the events in the vision Callum had shown me had actually taken place did not even occur to me at first. I had trusted Callum implicitly in life. That hadn't changed with his death.

As I mentally replayed the vision, I realised that I recognised not only Mary's father in the scene. The more I thought about it, the more one of the watching women seemed to resemble a much younger version of the woman who kept the village store. And one of the men holding the father was a youthful version of Martin from the tavern, but with an intelligent, sly face, much like the face of the old, bent man who had threatened to beat me with his cane and had called Martin an idiot.

There must have been well over a dozen villagers in the water, taking part in the murder of an entire family. Or if not actively participating, standing by, watching, without raising a murmur in protest.

I rose from the chair and wandered around the garden, trying to clear my mind of images of water rushing into an open mouth, of a nose splitting apart under impact, of a tiny clenched fist shimmering in dark dappled water.

I reached the rear wall and rested my arms upon it, staring out into the field, my gaze passing over the pond . . . and jerking back to it. The only reason that I hadn't realised sooner where the murders had taken place was because the body of water in the vision had looked so very different then. So much larger.

It was only then that another thought occurred to me and a small doubt appeared. I was certain that Callum believed the vision he had shown me to be of an event that had actually taken place. But what if he had been somehow deceived into believing it? Why someone or something should want me to see a scene that hadn't occurred was a question I couldn't even begin to answer, but I could now see a way of trying to establish the veracity of the vision.

Next to the privy in the garden stood a brick-built shed that Gwen called 'the outhouse'. Inside, from among a jumble of garden implements, I grabbed a spade, yanking it free and causing a minor avalanche of rakes and hoes. I ran back down the garden and vaulted the stile, spade in hand. A sense of urgency coursed through me; Ma and Gwen could return at any moment.

I slowed down as I neared the pond, approaching it almost warily. The weeks of uninterrupted sunshine had taken their toll: the area covered by water had shrunk to little more than a good-sized goldfish pond, surrounded by a bleached cracked expanse of baked mud. The remaining water stagnated in the centre of the dip in the land like an open festering wound. An odour similar to the smell that pervades a house after boiling cabbage hit me as I drew nearer the water's edge.

Placing the blade of the spade into the baked mud at the rim of the dip, I trod heavily upon it. I might as well have tried to dig concrete. Apart from raising a small cloud of dust, the spade made no impression upon the ground.

Moving further into the dip, towards the water and the smell, I lowered the spade once more. This time I sensed there was some give lower down, though the blade again made little impression on the surface.

Stepping closer to the water's edge, trying to ignore what at this range was becoming a stench, I inserted the edge of the blade into a crack in the mud and concentrated all my weight into a downward shove delivered through my right boot. The blade sliced through the solid surface and into softer ground beneath. With a grunt of effort, I levered away a chunk of baked white clay. Beneath this iron exterior the mud was the consistency of stiff dough and browner, like mud ought to be.

Pausing only to swipe away sweat from my eyes with the back of my hand, I quickly cleared the top crust to form a rough circle a few feet in diameter. Then I started to dig down.

It was easy at first. It wasn't until I had dug a hole about three feet deep that the going began to get tougher. The mud became wet and heavy, and slurped as I heaved it out. Water seeped from the sides of the hole and filled the bottom with thick sludge. The mud was now the colour of dark faeces and smelled nearly as foul.

Apart from half a brick and a lump of unidentifiable pulp that may have been the remains of a log, I found nothing.

I moved right to the water's edge to stand in the area that must have held the deepest water when the pond was five or six times, or more, its current size thirty years earlier.

The mud here had not baked solid and digging was easier initially. But I had gone down barely a foot when the hole began to fill with brown slurry like chocolate porridge.

I pulled off my shirt and dug as though my life depended upon it. I didn't pause to flick away gnats that drank the sweat pouring freely down my chest and back. A mound of glistening, smelly muck formed by my side as I thrust the spade into the hole again and again. I shovelled fast enough to stay ahead of the sludge seeping from the sides of the ever-deepening hole, but at a price. The muscles in my arms and back burned like overheated wires and my breathing grew hoarse and shallow in the hot air. I could not keep up the pace for much longer, but dared not slow in the knowledge that the ingressing water would defeat me.

A dull clang reverberated as the spade struck a stone and sent shock waves up my tired arms. Before the sludge enveloped it, I could see that the stone was sizeable, more a small rock. I renewed my efforts and revealed the edges. Throwing the spade to one side, I knelt at the hole's rim and lowered my arms. My groping fingers found the edge of the rock and I heaved, muscles protesting fiercely. With a burp and a slurp, the rock lifted and came free of the cloying earth. With the last of my strength I tilted it and let it fall against the side of the hole, standing on end. More slurry oozed into the cavity vacated by the rock, filling it, but not before I glimpsed something that had been lying beneath the rock.

I thrust my right hand into the deepening sludge, feeling around until my fingers located a hard object. It was embedded firmly in the mud and I had to work my tired arm some more to wriggle my fingers under it. I tugged and the object moved slightly. Ignoring the pain in my abused muscles, I gave a heave and the object came free in my hand.

It was caked in dirt to the extent that I could not describe it other than as being curved; a little like a boomerang but smaller, the curve more pronounced. I stepped around the hole and bent to the pond, wrinkling my nose against the stench. I lowered the object into the foul water and swooshed it back and fore, washing the mud away.

When I lifted my hand from the water, the thing I held in my hand was a creamy, light yellow colour like faded parchment. A row of protrusions that jutted from its top rim were a mix of off-white, deeper yellow and orangey-brown. Irregular gaps suggested missing protrusions.

Divested of its muddy coating, the object was unmistakable. It was the lower jawbone of a human being.

Foreboding

The following afternoon I almost ran to the Glade in my eagerness to meet Mary. I made myself walk because I did not want to arrive in her presence in a bath of sweat. As it was, I was covered in a fine sheen of perspiration, like early morning dew, by the time I reached the Glade. Mary was there before me, lying on the grass humming a cheerful tune.

I crept forward, knelt and placed a kiss upon her lips. Her arms encircled my neck as she returned the kiss and slipped her tongue between my teeth.

We pulled apart a little breathlessly.

"You could at least have opened your eyes to make sure it was me," I said in mock indignation.

She giggled and turned towards me. Once more I was stunned by the depth and beauty of her eyes. The eyes of heroines in Disney animated films—always disproportionately large and almond-shaped—could have been modelled on Mary's. But hers were better; they were real and they sparkled for me.

"Who else would make such a commotion?" she said. "I could hear you approaching half a mile away. Dainty on your feet you're not." She laughed. "Your kissing makes up for it though. So . . . what are you waiting for?"

I needed no second invitation and sank back into her embrace. When we eventually broke apart again, we both breathed heavily.

"Um. . . ." I said. "Shall we, er, I mean, do you want to . . . um. . . ."

"Cross the stream?" A mischievous grin played across her lips that were suffused a ruby red.

I blushed but did not lower my gaze. "Yes. Let's go back to that circle of trees and . . . and rip each other's clothes off. If you want to."

"Try stopping me."

I bounded to my feet and grabbed her hands to haul her up. This time neither of us paused to remove our footwear. Still clasping hands, we ran across the stream, laughing as cold water splashed up our legs.

We reached the circle of trees and forced our way between the leafy boughs, barely noticing the stings as whip-like branches sprang back into place as we passed.

Gaining the grassy centre of the ring of trees, we paused for a moment. We gazed deep into each other's eyes and smiled.

Then we fell upon and devoured each other like savages.

Unlike the first time we made love, I can recall with perfect clarity every inflamed moment as every inch of her body became mine, and mine hers. But some memories are too private, too cherished, to share.

Afterwards we lay naked in each other's arms and talked into the early evening. By unspoken consent, we avoided discussing events in the village. Instead we talked of happy times. I told her tales of my childhood in Newcastle: attending football matches with Da and Callum; being forced to dress in girl's clothes by Morfydd and parade before her giggling friends; Ma drinking too much sherry at Christmas and having us in stitches with her uncharacteristically ribald jokes.

Mary spoke of her younger days: jaunts in the countryside with her aunt; visits to the Baileys' farm to see the animals; rare joyous occasions involving her father.

We discussed an imaginary future together. Where we would live: a rose-covered cottage by the sea where Mary would teach me to swim. How many children we would have: three girls, two boys. What we would do for a living as we grew old together: Mary would become a famous artist, I a groundsman at a football club.

That long afternoon, lying in cool grass under a hot summer sun, was probably the happiest I have ever been.

As the evening drew in and the heat went out of the day, we cuddled closer. Then we made love for the third and last time. It was also the best. We were tender, loving, generous, giving and taking but not forcing or demanding.

Later we talked some more, bodies entwined, until the sun sank below the trees.

By the time we made our reluctant way back to the village, night had fallen. The moon was big and bright and lit our way in its cold milky light.

We halted at the edge of the village and kissed. I held Mary tightly around her waist, unwilling to let her go.

She smiled and kissed me again. "Silly," she said. "You'll see me again soon."

"I know," I said. "It's just that I love you Mary Fletcher. More than I could ever love anyone. I would lay down my life for you." I meant it too, or at least thought I did.

"I love you too John Andrews," she murmured.

I buried my face in the dark mane of her hair, breathing in her aroma as we hugged farewell. Then we kissed once more, long and lingering, the kiss of lovers. I will never forget the silky texture of her lips and sweetness of her tongue.

It was our final kiss.

August appeared like July's twin sister, hot, sultry and cloudless. Of course, we didn't know it at the time but the heatwave would only last another two weeks. By the middle of August dark clouds had rolled in from the Atlantic. Brilliant blue skies and sweltering temperatures would become a pleasant memory as rain arrived and remained pretty much until the following spring.

It was on the second day of the month when events in Tregeagle came to a head. It was the day that shaped the rest of my life. A Friday.

I awoke that morning with a sense of foreboding that I could not shake and that grew stronger throughout the day. A vague feeling of unease that something bad was about to happen, like a dog sensing an approaching thunder storm. The weather was particularly close and oppressive, which did nothing to lighten my spirits.

After finishing my chores, I headed for the Glade in hope of seeing Mary. We hadn't arranged to meet again for another couple of days but I went on the off chance of her being there. The Glade was deserted. I sat for a while but felt too restless to settle. The sense of approaching danger grew stronger by the hour, but I had no idea from where the danger came.

I headed back to Black Tops. I wanted to be close to Ma to protect her if necessary from the unknown peril.

Ma and Gwen were in the kitchen preparing lunch. I announced that they would have the pleasure of my company that lunchtime. Ma raised her eyebrows. Gwen, of course, had to make a comment.

"Not stepping out with young Mary today, Johnny Boy? Lover's tiff is it?" She grinned.

I sighed good-naturedly. I was well used to my aunt's teasing by now. "No," I said. "I'm seeing Mary the day after tomorrow. She doesn't like to—or at least can't—leave her father every day. I thought it would be nice for us to have a family lunch together for a change."

"Aye," said Gwen, eyes a-twinkle. "Come have a nibble with us. There's plenty of time to nibble on Mary Fletcher."

She managed it every time. My ears glowed as the blush spread like wildfire and Gwen's delighted grin grew even wider.

"Hush, Gwen," said Ma before her sister could pipe up again. "It will be lovely to all have lunch together. Sit yourself down boy."

So I sat and ate lunch with my mother and aunt. They were in good spirits and my mood lifted somewhat. However the gnawing feeling of impending doom could not be completely dispelled.

After lunch, Gwen disappeared without a word as Ma and I washed the dishes.

"Phew! This is one of the hottest days yet," said Ma, dabbing at her brow.

"Aye," I agreed. "Probably *the* hottest."

"Any plans this afternoon, love?"

"Nothing special. Thought I'd just flop about and melt."

"Well, how about us finding some shade in the garden and catching up on some reading?"

I agreed readily enough. The heat of the afternoon was too sapping to even think about expending energy. So I carried two chairs from the kitchen into the back garden and placed them in the shade. We settled down and opened our books.

My latest book from Gwen's collection was *The Old Curiosity Shop*. In truth I was finding it a little hard going. As I struggled with the innocence of Little Nell and the lecherous antics of Quilp, my eyes strayed often from the print to glance towards the garden wall and the pond beyond.

Ma sat beside me sighing as she turned the pages of a historical romance. She must have glanced up and caught me staring into the distance.

"Anything wrong, *cariad?*"

"No, Ma, I'm fine. Just thinking, that's all."

"Hmm . . . nothing to do with that pond is it?"

I looked at her sharply. "Why do you ask that?"

"Well, when me and Gwen were out the other day, somebody dug some holes at the edge of that pond. Either that or there's some bloody big aquatic moles in that field."

I thought I had done a thorough job of filling in the holes after I had dropped the jawbone back in. Obviously not thorough enough to fool the eagle-eyed sisters.

I sighed. "It was me."

"Why, love?"

"Um, would you believe that I was digging for worms, you know, to go fishing?"

Ma snorted. "Fishing! I suppose you were going to fashion a rod from a branch and use cotton for line, were you? You wouldn't know a fish's head from its arse."

"Tail, Ma, tail."

"Whatever. Come on, my boy. What were you really doing?"

Ma placed her book face down in her lap and half turned in her chair so that she could look at me face-on. I knew her too well. She wouldn't let this go until I had given her a satisfactory answer.

"I was looking for something. But I can't tell you what. I don't want to get you involved."

"Did you find what you were looking for?"

"Yes."

Her next question took me by surprise. "Has this anything to do with Callum?"

"Callum? How can it have anything to do with him?"

She was silent for a few moments but continued to look at me intently.

"He comes to me in my dreams," she said. "He tells me things. Some of them I don't like."

"Ma, are you all right?"

"Pah! Don't look at me as if I'm going mad. I'm not the only one around here who has vivid dreams. I've seen you some mornings, yawning your head off as if you've not slept a wink. Very distracted you seem. A lot on your mind." She nodded slowly, knowingly.

I've said it before and I'll say it again: a wily old bird was my mother.

"What has Cal said to you?" I asked.

"Lots of things. I can talk back to him in my dreams." Her tone became wistful. "We speak of Newcastle and your Da and sister. *Duw*, I miss them John."

"I know, Ma. So do I."

She went on, her tone harder. "I don't understand some of the things he tells me. Some of it is about you. He told me to make sure you wear his medallion. He told me not to interfere in whatever's going on with you."

"He's right enough there. It really has nothing to do with me. At least, I've done nothing to cause it. But please, Ma, don't worry about it. I think it will soon be over. And I'm sure that I'm quite safe." I tried to sound reassuring but sounded more like I was trying to convince myself. Unease still simmered below the surface like a festering boil.

"At least tell me this, John. Do *you* dream about Callum? Does he talk to you?"

I nodded. "But it's more than just dreams. I go to a place, Ma. It's a sunny meadow with thick grass and buttercups. It seems so *real*. It's a wonderful place." I omitted to mention the time that it had not been so wonderful, when it had been icily cold and occupied by Mitch Mahoney. "I meet Callum there. I can touch him and he's warm. I know I'm asleep when I'm with him, yet I'm *there* too. It sounds crazy . . . I thought at first I was going mad. But I know that I'm not, Ma." I paused, collecting my thoughts. Ma waited as though she knew I had more to say. "I've missed Callum so much these last seven years. Seeing him again in the Meadow has helped. But I don't think I'll see much more of him. He'll be passing on, as he calls it, very soon. I may get chance to say goodbye to him. I think I'll be able to cope with losing him again. Maybe... maybe I'll even be comforted knowing that he's moved on. . . ." I tailed off, my vision blurring.

"What about your father and Morfydd? Have you seen them at this Meadow?"

I shook my head, causing tears to run down my cheeks. I swiped them away, angry for allowing myself to cry in front of my mother. "Cal said they passed straight on. Be glad that they did, Ma. Callum doesn't always inhabit the Meadow. Most of the time he's in a place he calls Darkland. It sounds a horrible place. But he won't be there much longer. He'll soon be with Da and Morfydd. Perhaps me and you will be one day too."

"I have never doubted that for one second." Ma smiled and her eyes glistened. She dabbed at them with a tissue that she always seemed to have somewhere about her person. "Let me ask one last question, John. This thing that's happening, does it have anything to do with Tregeagle?"

I nodded. "Ma, this village is . . . *wrong*."

"I know. I feel that too. Well, me and your Auntie Gwen have been talking. We both want to return to Wales. Something's going on here with your aunt, though she won't tell me what. I'm not stupid or deaf. I've heard some queer goings-on from her bedroom in the still of night. I think that has something to do with this accursed place too. I want to be gone from here. I want to go home."

"Home? Newcastle . . . but you said Wales?"

"Wales is my home, John. It's where my heart lies."

"Oh."

"Don't look so forlorn, boy. Newcastle will always hold a special place in my heart. Your Da, Callum, Morfydd . . . but it wasn't the same without them. No longer home." She sat straighter, her jaw jutting out in a look I was familiar with when she was in determined mood. "Nope, my mind's made up. And Gwen agrees with me. Arthur

Bailey's given her a lift to town on his trap. She's contacting the owners of Black Top to give up the tenancy. And she's posting a letter to our cousin in Wales to ask that she arrange some accommodation for us from the beginning of September."

My mind raced. I had known that we wouldn't be staying in Tregeagle indefinitely, but to be suddenly told that I had just four more weeks to spend with Mary . . .

"What's wrong, John? I thought you'd be glad to leave here sooner than later."

"I will be glad to leave this place, it's just—"

"Is it Mary? Are you that serious about her?"

I looked my mother squarely in the eyes. "I'm in love with her, Ma. I don't want to leave her. I *can't* leave her."

"Well, well. I certainly must meet this young lady." Ma hesitated for a moment, then: "Why don't you ask her to come with us?"

"It's her father. I don't think he'd let her leave."

"Hmm . . . Gwen's mentioned *him* to me. Sounds a nasty piece of work. Let me talk to Gwen. I'm sure we can come up with something."

I felt a surge of relief that almost washed away the foreboding that lay heavy on me like a shroud. Ma and Gwen probably would have come up with a solution too. They made a very formidable pair that might even have been a match for someone like Frank Fletcher. Diminutive in stature they were, but giants at heart.

Friday wore on and the feeling of oppression grew within me.

Gwen returned as the sun was setting, looking drawn yet at the same time buoyant. She said little over supper and retired to bed immediately afterwards. Ma soon followed.

During supper, I had also been quiet, only picking at my food. The air of expectancy was so strong that I could almost taste it. A ball of dread had settled in my stomach like a stodgy meal.

I took a large, well-trimmed oil-lamp to my bedroom and set it down on the windowsill. I turned it low, but did not extinguish the flame. Then I sat fully dressed in a chair next to the open window. Folding my arms, I settled down to wait.

How sleep found me I will never know. I felt as taut with tension as a fully wound spring. But find me it did for next thing I knew I was blinking in the bright sunlight of the Meadow.

I turned to greet Callum. There he stood as large as life, a serious expression on his face. He returned my embrace but hurriedly, as though time was short.

"Hello, John," he said. "Our destiny is nigh."

"I know," I said. "I've felt it all day. I'm scared, Cal."

"Fear can be a good thing. I'm scared too."

"You! Scared?"

He nodded, the serious expression never leaving his face. "I used to be scared a lot before . . . when I was alive. That time I fought Mitch I was afraid. The first time I went into battle in the war I was almost petrified with fear."

"What are you afraid of now, Cal?"

"When I return to Darkland, Mitch will be waiting for me. And there will be others. This time when we fight there's a lot at stake. At least one life, a real life, depends upon the outcome." He shook his head as I opened my mouth to ask a question. "I can say little more about it. But I am afraid that I will fail."

"Cal, please be careful. And . . . kick Mitch's arse!"

At last Callum smiled, but it was gone almost as soon as it had appeared. "I will try my best. I can do no more. But I am also afraid for you, little brother. *You* must be careful."

"But they're just ghosts, Cal. Lost souls. They can't hurt me . . . can they?"

"Yes, they can hurt you. They can kill you and they will attempt to.

You must not let them. Ma needs you."

"Then I'll run. Take Ma and Gwen and Mary. Leave Tregeagle."

My brother shook his head sadly. "It's too late for flight. Didn't I say that our destiny is nigh?"

"If we leave now, the moment I wake up, we'll be safe. I can persuade Ma and—"

"John! You're not listening. Running away is no longer an option, if it ever was." He glanced around at the rolling grass. "We must leave this place now, perhaps for the last time. My love goes with you, little brother."

He paused, head cocked to one side as though listening. I could hear nothing. When he spoke again, it was with a note of great urgency.

"Go now! It has arrived. The peril is upon you!"

The Storm Breaks

I awoke with a start, adrenaline already coursing through my body. Two things I noticed immediately. The Dead Lights were abroad, flooding the bedroom with their cold blue glow that overpowered the flickering gleam of the lamp. The second thing I noticed was that my bed was occupied.

My breath hitched in my chest as I stared at the occupant. I recognised her immediately from the vision Callum had shown me. Not the young girl who had visited me previously, but her mother. Long fair hair clung to her scalp, wet and bedraggled. Nose mangled and splayed from the vicious blow I had watched a man deliver as she struggled to escape her captors while her daughter was being drowned by Frank Fletcher. Her face was caked not with blood but with mud, tendrils of weed caught around her ears and in her hair. The eyes of the woman in the vision had blazed with terror and frustration. The eyes of the creature lying in my bed glinted with malevolence and cunning.

She—it—began to move, sitting up and starting to slide towards the foot of the bed. The sheet and blanket that covered the bed, and the creature to the waist, began to ruck and crumple as it moved.

I jumped to my feet and looked around wildly. My glance fell outside the window, judging the distance to the ground and dismissing it as a possible escape route except as a final resort. As my glance moved back up, something else caught my eye that momentarily drove all other considerations clean from my mind.

A person stood in the field beyond the rear garden wall. The person faced away from me, silhouetted by the deep blue glow emanating from the pond. But I would have known her anywhere. I even recognised the dress she wore; the same white one she had worn the day we first made love.

I yelled through the open window: "Mary! Don't move! I'm coming!" I have no idea whether she heard me. There was no head movement or change in posture to suggest that she had. But I had no time to worry about it or shout again. The sound of rustling movement from behind me demanded my undivided attention. I spun around.

While I had been diverted, the mother-creature had moved to the foot of the bed. It was fortuitous indeed that the bed had been made and that the creature had materialised, or however the hell it had arrived, *beneath* the bedclothes. The sheet and blanket hampered its movements but it was almost clear of them. It was barely a few feet away from me and was starting to swing its legs from under the bedclothes to gain the floor. A sopping ragged skirt rode up to reveal mud-flecked thighs with fish-belly white skin. An expression of eager lust animated the slack skin of the face.

Its bare feet gained the floor and I heard a sound like water sloshing in a half-empty barrel as it stood. I became vaguely aware of a tingling sensation in my groin as my testicles attempted to withdraw into my body.

The creature opened its mouth.

"Jo-hn. . . ." That awful crypt whisper and charnel house waft of breath—it sounded and smelled just like its daughter.

It held out its arms and took a wet shuffling step towards me. Another step or two and I would be in its embrace.

I feinted to move to my right but side-stepped smartly to my left and bolted for the door. A hiss of foul air followed me but I easily made it to the door. Had I not been able to beat the creature over five yards, I would have deserved everything it could offer me. It had, after all, been dead for nigh on thirty years and carried a fair amount of excess water judging by the sloshing sound as it shuffled after me.

I wrenched open the door and exited sharply, yanking the door closed behind me. Then I realised my mistake. The bedroom had been brightly illuminated by the Dead Lights and I hadn't thought to grab the oil-lamp as I fled. Closing the door had shuttered me into pitch blackness.

Disorientated, heart racing, I stood uncertainly. It was only when I heard something thud against my bedroom door that I moved again. Without any clear idea of what I was doing, I stumbled across the landing, hands held out before me like a blind man, until I blundered into what felt like another door. By the direction I thought I'd taken, this must be Ma's bedroom.

I fumbled for the door handle and grasped it gratefully. I thrust open the door and stumbled across the threshold. It took me a moment to take in the unexpected sight that opened before me. For a start, the room was lit by another blue glow, like that of the Dead Lights, but I was now at the front of the house and heavy drapes covered the window. The next realisation was that I was in Gwen's room, not Ma's, and my aunt was once again not alone.

A figure stood at the foot of Gwen's bed. A figure of a man. A blue, glowing man. Gwen was crouched near the headboard, bedclothes pinched into a tight knot at her chest by the fierce grip of her hands. She stared at the apparition with a blend of emotions playing across her face: dread, awe and, I am quite certain, supplication.

The man was elderly. He turned his head towards me and I knew that I was looking upon the ghost of my maternal grandfather, a man I had never met during his lifetime. His expression was melancholy, a marked contrast to the woman in my bedroom. As far as I could tell, this visitor held no malicious intent. Besides, the figure looked like a ghost is traditionally supposed to look: vague and insubstantial. I could see my aunt's wardrobe through the blue shimmering figure. If it did hold evil designs on my aunt, I couldn't see how it could carry them out.

The woman-thing trying to escape my bedroom was a different story. It looked solid and perfectly capable of implementing the injurious intent it carried in its eyes. I knew that I needed to lead it away from Ma and Gwen.

With one last wondering glance at my dead grandfather, I backed out of my aunt's bedroom, pulling the door tightly shut. Strangely, I was not thrust back into pitch blackness, the reason for which became apparent as soon as I whirled round to face the landing. My bedroom door was half open. A mud-smeared arm had appeared and was pulling the door wider, allowing more cold blue light to spill into the landing.

Without waiting for more of the woman-thing to appear, I scooted past my bedroom to the top of the stairs. Another blast of rotten air assailed my nostrils as I passed my widening bedroom door. I took the stairs two at a time for the stretch that I could see, only slowing at the lower reaches that remained in darkness.

No light from my bedroom reached the downstairs hallway. I felt my way along the wall, knowing that once I could open the kitchen door the Dead Lights would enable me to see. My ears strained for the sound of sloshing footsteps following me downstairs, but I could hear nothing.

I paused, wondering why I could not hear any sound of pursuit. Maybe it wouldn't follow me downstairs but would head for Ma's or Gwen's bedrooms. Torn between wanting to rush to Mary and not wanting to leave my family in possible danger, I dithered.

It was probably mere moments that I stood inactive, but realisation that I was neither helping Mary nor my family got me moving again. I turned and, heedless of the darkness, ran back to the stairs and up them, half-expecting at any moment to fall into the clutch of something damp and icily cold.

I gained the landing. My bedroom door was half open, blue light still spilling through and lighting up the empty landing. Both Ma's and Gwen's bedroom doors were closed.

Without any more hesitation, I ran to Ma's door and burst into her bedroom. It was in darkness and she was alone. Ma sat up, bleary-eyed, blinking at me groggily.

"Ma!" I said loudly. "Go to Gwen's room. No time to explain."

I didn't wait to see if she'd obey my instruction. Turning on one heel, I ran to my bedroom and thrust the door wide. The Dead Lights were shining more powerfully than I had seen before and the whole room was lit up like an operating theatre. There was no sign of the woman-thing.

In a few strides, I crossed to the window and looked out. Mary stood where I had last seen her, but something was wrong. Something about the way she stood, swaying slightly as though in water. Yet she was nowhere near the pond. I knew from my recent excavations precisely where the pond began and it was at least another ten yards beyond where Mary stood.

There was no time to stare and puzzle. I had to get to her.

I ran back onto the landing. Ma was just appearing in her bedroom doorway, shrugging on her dressing gown. I ignored her and descended the stairs at a gallop, not slowing towards the bottom where the Dead Lights failed to reach.

Placing one hand on the wall, the other held stiffly out in front of me, I trotted down the hallway until my fingers bent against the kitchen door.

The heavy wooden door swung open and I was once more bathed in cold blue light. I ran to the back door, suffused with a sense of urgency so strong it verged on panic. I struggled to undo the bolt and latch, with each passing second becoming more and more certain that the girl I loved was facing some grave danger alone.

At last the door yielded and I was through it and away across the garden. Although the rear wall blocked out the Dead Lights at ground level, they were bright enough to light up the garden like a flare and I was vaguely aware of a kerfuffle coming from the disturbed animals and poultry as I sprinted past them. I barely paused as I reached the wall and vaulted the stile. Then I came to a dead halt in disbelief.

The blue glow was powerful this close to its source and the field was clearly illuminated by the incandescent light. What had been little more than a large brown puddle in a patchwork of cracked mud, the pond had expanded to fill the broad dip in the land. The water shimmered, both giving off and reflecting the Dead Lights. Blue inky water covered an area perhaps ten times larger or more than when I had retired to my bedroom. It now resembled a small lake.

My mind balked. Despite all that I had witnessed over the past couple of months—my late brother and the equally late Mitch Mahoney, abominations of a dead girl and her equally dead mother, the spirit of my grandfather—and had accepted reluctantly as the truth, howsoever bizarre, my senses refused to accept this latest perversion of reality. The rational part of my mind exerted dominance and insisted that I must be hallucinating.

Mary stood up to her thighs in water, a few yards in from the water's edge: the new expanded edge that I was certain could not exist. As I stood rooted to the spot in denial, she began to move slowly forward towards the centre. The skirt of her dress floated out behind her like a bridal train. Where the water lapped higher at her waist, the dress material became transparent, sticking to the smooth, unblemished skin beneath.

It was this detail that made me move. If I was in the midst of a hallucination, it was a mightily powerful one to the point of allowing me to imagine Mary's dress becoming see-through as it became wet. As I ran forward I reasoned, if that is the correct word for considerations so patently irrational, that if I could accept the Meadow as real in the sense that my subconscious self actually went there, then accepting that a pond could increase in size tenfold in a few hours at the height of a drought was not too much of a mental leap.

As I closed the twenty yards or so from the wall to the water's edge—that afternoon it would have been more like fifty yards—I shouted to Mary to stop. She must have been close enough to have heard me but she did not react. She continued to walk, *wade*, slowly but steadfastly outwards as if she were sleepwalking.

I hesitated for only a second when I reached the water's edge before stepping into her wake. The water was cold and splashed up my legs, silencing for good that rational part of my mind that had refused to believe the evidence of my own eyes. Although the gradient of the hollow was gentle, the water was up to my waist by the time I reached Mary and I was having to swing my arms forwards to move through it at any speed. We were only about halfway to the middle of the pool and I suspected that the depth in the very centre would be sufficient to completely immerse us.

Mary halted when I grabbed her arm, but did not turn. I swung her gently around to face me. She did not resist. Her eyes were open but staring into an unseen distance and glazed as though in a trance. I took hold of her other arm too and shook her, talking to her, babbling, desperate to glimpse a look of recognition in her face. Nothing. She stared straight ahead, unseeing, expression blank.

I scooped up a handful of water and splashed it into her face. And another. With a start and a gasp, Mary's eyes widened and focused, and she rocked back on her heels. I caught her arm again to prevent her tipping backwards. Mary's head turned from side to side, trying to take in her surroundings. Lines of bewilderment creased the flawless skin of her forehead.

"John. . . ." she managed. "Where . . . what am I doing here?"

My mouth had barely started to form an answer when my words died in my throat. Both out heads turned towards the centre of the pool.

A patch of water about a yard or so away from us had begun to bubble violently like the surface of a whirlbath or the boiling surface commotion caused by a shoal of feeding piranha.

It would have been a good idea to have backed rapidly from the water at that point, but I was too scared to move and there probably wouldn't have been time to get far. For a moment or two later, something erupted from the centre of the boiling patch of water. We were both drenched in spray as whatever it was landed in front of us with a violent splash.

Blinking water from my eyes, I peered at it. It stood midriff-deep in the pool and regarded us coldly.

It came as no surprise that I recognised it. I had seen it, too, in Callum's vision when it had been a man, not a thing. A man whose children were being horribly murdered before his eyes. Mary and I stood face to face with the embodiment of Mr Flynn.

It glared at us from those now familiar baleful red and black eyes that seemed to run in the family or at least the family's afterlife version. Obligatory strands of weed were entwined in thick dripping black hair. The pallid face bore evidence of a beating that Callum's vision hadn't shown me and it held its head at an odd angle as though its neck had been broken. Perhaps that had been the only way they had been able to subdue the frantic father sufficiently to drown him. Despite my fear and revulsion, I almost pitied the creature.

It grinned: a lopsided, grisly travesty of a grin, like the smile of a murderous clown. Mary shrieked, a high note of panic, and her hand scrabbled wildly at my side. I grabbed it in mine and held it tight. Then slowly and carefully, not taking my eyes from the late Mr Flynn, I began to back away, tugging Mary along with me. It followed us with its noxious gaze but made no move to wade after us. That puzzled me, but only for a moment.

We had backed up three or four steps when I heard the sound behind me. Another bubbling noise. I let go of Mary and only half-turned towards it; I was not about to present my back to Mr Flynn.

Another patch of water, smaller than the first, bubbled violently as if an underwater volcano was erupting. Through the bubbles burst a small figure, that of a child. The Flynn boy. It grinned inanely and I could not help but notice the gaps between its infant teeth and the discoloured stained appearance of the teeth that were present. I wondered briefly if it had been the boy's jawbone I had unearthed.

The boy stood between us and the edge of the pool where the water was shallower, yet it still reached his chest, so pitifully young had he been when his life was snatched away.

I glanced back at Mary. She looked dumbstruck with fear and had started to back away from the monstrosities. The only trouble was, she was also moving away from me.

"Mary! Stop!"

She glanced at me but switched her gaze back to Mr Flynn and then to the boy, darting between the two things as she continued to move away from them. And me.

"Come back towards me!" I cried, my gaze mimicking hers as I made sure neither of the creatures was moving.

It must have taken every ounce of courage she possessed, but she obeyed. She waded back to me and I hugged her thankfully. Still facing her, I took both her hands in mine and waded backwards, parallel with the pool's shore. My intention was to skirt around the boy-thing and regain dry land as soon as we were clear of it.

We had barely made two yards when the water over my shoulder started to gurgle and froth. From beneath the surface emerged something I was already acquainted with. What had once been a nine-year-old girl smiled in what might have been mistaken for a friendly fashion if not for the glint of malice in the fathomless eyes.

Mary froze and stared at the girl-thing. A high keening whimper came from Mary's throat. I don't think she was even aware that she was making the sound.

There was only one direction left for us to take and that was to retrace our steps and reach dry land on the other side of the boy. This is what we started to do, Mary walking backwards with me guiding her. But I knew we were wasting our time; it seemed obvious to me what would happen next.

Sure enough, as we reached the point between father and son from where we had started our curious dance, turbulence broke out in the calm patch of water behind Mary and up popped Mrs Flynn. The only scant consolation was that if the creature was here, it could not be in Black Tops shuffling after Ma and Gwen.

By now my mind had passed beyond utter terror into the area of calm that lies beyond on the rim of the bottomless pit of insanity. When Mrs Flynn erupted from the pool, I felt a mad urge to laugh that I only managed to quell because it was clear from the expression of abject terror on Mary's face that her mind was also hovering on the brink of madness. The slightest nudge—hearing me laugh, for instance—might push her irrevocably over the edge.

As it was, Mary must have read my expression for she glanced wildly behind her and her shoulders sagged. It was the sight of what the former Mrs Flynn held in its arms that, I believe, finally tipped Mary's balance. Clutched to its chest, swaddled in sopping limp rags, was the baby. It regarded us with the same malevolent gaze as its parents and siblings. Alien eyes, evil and all-knowing, in the face of an infant. The ultimate abomination. Utter desolation of innocence.

The mother-thing opened its mouth and spoke in that deathly whisper I'd heard earlier. "Ma-ry . . . Ma-ry . . . Ma-ry. . . ." Over and over.

Mary looked back at me and I felt as though my heart would burst. Her jaw had dropped, slack, and a line of spittle drooled from her lips unheeded. Her eyes were still alert, but something had departed her gaze. It had become somehow feral.

Frantically, I searched for a way out. The shortest path to shore was also the least heavily guarded. Only the Flynn boy, little more than a toddler, stood between us and dry land.

Mary's head was turned away from me, towards the baby. "Mary," I said softly. No reaction. "Mary!" Nothing. "MARY!"

Her shoulders jerked and she turned her head my way. Her face was now a slack mask of utter dejection. I shouted at her again: "MARY, GRAB MY HAND!"

My yell must have pierced the fog that enveloped her for she started to move towards me. But she moved like an automaton, no haste or purpose, as though her brain was in neutral.

I glanced back at the toddler. It hadn't moved but stood regarding us with an expression of malice, ancient and incongruous in such a young-looking face.

Quickly turning my head, I could see that none of the other members of the Flynn clan had made any move towards us. A small bloom of hope dared blossom in my chest.

We might yet escape.

Vengeance

Standing waist-deep in inky water, washed in the cerulean glow of the Dead Lights, I beckoned Mary to me. I stole a final glance at the toddler, sizing it up, knowing that I could trample over it to reach the shore.

The glance was a mistake. It allowed Mrs Flynn to guess my intent. With a sibilant cry of rage, it flung the bundle in its arms contemptuously to one side. The baby disappeared briefly from view, only to bob back to the surface almost immediately. It floated on its side and turned its head towards us, the lapping water failing to douse the red spark that glowed within the endless blackness of its eyes.

"Quick Mary! Give me your hand!" I took a step towards her and stretched out my arm.

She was too slow. The mother closed the few yards to Mary with terrifying speed, slicing through the water like the blade of an oar rather than the cumbersome lurch I had to employ. With a hiss of triumph, it caught hold of Mary by one arm and started to pull her towards the deeper water. Mary grimaced, which gave me hope that her mind had not gone completely, but did nothing to resist.

I lunged forward and grabbed her other arm. For a few crazed moments, the late Mrs Flynn and I engaged in a tug-of-war using Mary as the rope. My extra weight and strength told and Mary began to move back towards me and the water's edge. As soon as she was close enough for me to grab around the waist, I let go of her arm with my left hand, while still gripping her with my right. But so engrossed had I been in my tugging match with Mrs Flynn, I had momentarily forgotten about the others.

Before I could wrap my left arm around Mary's waist, it was seized above the wrist in a tight grip so icy cold my hand immediately went numb. I gasped and jerked my head sideways, almost banging heads with Mr Flynn.

Its fetid breath came over me in waves and I almost swooned. Its oddly-angled throat worked as it tried to speak. All it could manage was one word that it croaked like a hoarse toad: "Fle—tcher. . . ."

Without wasting any more time in idle chit-chat, the creature leaned back and tugged on my arm.

Now I was in trouble. My right hand clung desperately to Mary's hand. The mother-thing resumed its steady pulling on Mary's other arm. I struggled to tug my left arm free of Mr Flynn's clutches. It was hopeless. The creature's grip was so vice-like and chilling that my arm was now numb to the elbow.

We moved slowly back towards the centre of the pool. I struggled as only a dying man can, but to no avail. I was rapidly weakening and we gained speed as the creatures, perhaps sensing my frailty, increased the strain. Now the feeling in my entire left arm had gone and my right hand ached from the desperate grip that I was just about managing to maintain upon Mary. Her arms must have been nearly popping from their sockets, but she appeared to have passed beyond any comprehension of what was happening and made no effort to try to halt our forward momentum.

Summoning my last reserves of energy, I concentrated all my weight into a backward lunge, at the same instant digging the heels of my boots into the muddy floor of the pool. Our forward motion halted. The creatures spat like angry cats and tried to yank us forward again, but my heels had dug in securely and anchored us, though I had to strain every sinew to hold us in place.

Encouraged by my tiny victory, I gathered myself for one last superhuman effort. I would drag Mary and, if necessary, the late Mr and Mrs Flynn to dry land.

In the instant before I started to heave myself backwards, I felt something cold and hard thrust painfully into my lower back. I gasped in surprise and straightened. Sensing my distraction, the adult creatures renewed their efforts and we started to slide forward once more.

As I tried in vain to dig my heels back in—my boots merely threw up clouds of silt as they slid through the mud—I glanced behind me. The girl and boy creatures were floating behind, their hands thrust against my back. The water was too deep for them to stand and so they could not push me effectively; the initial touch of their hands had been enough to break my concentration and allow their parents to regain the advantage.

Before despair overcame me, I yanked and struggled, but ineffectually. The water was now up to my chest and would soon lap against my chin. It had already reached Mary's neck.

Both my arms had grown numb with fatigue and the deathly chill of Flynn's grasp. A burning sensation began in my chest, vague at first but rapidly increasing in intensity. *A heart attack* I thought with disinterest. I became more interested as I realised the heat was coming from outside my body.

Then understanding lit up my mind like a flare. Callum's St Christopher medallion, dangling from its chain beneath my shirt, vibrated like something alive. Where it touched my chest, the skin tingled and singed.

I had no time to wonder why the medallion was tingling or what use I could put it to. All I had time to think was use it I must. There was one major obstacle. To reach inside my shirt and grasp the medallion, I would have to free one of my hands. My left hand was useless, grasped in an unbreakable sub-zero vice. My right hand gripped Mary.

We were barely yards from the pool's centre. Water lapped around my shoulders. It had reached Mary's chin and was already slopping between her slack lips. The only factor in our favour was that our rate of progress had slowed significantly as we reached deeper water and the creatures' purchase on the pond floor lessened. Nevertheless, if I didn't act immediately we would both be dead.

I let go of Mary's hand. She surged further ahead as the counterweight of my resistance was removed. The eyes of Mrs Flynn pulsed red with triumph.

Ignoring the urge to shake feeling back into my aching hand and wrist, I thrust them inside my shirt and grabbed the St Christopher. Instant warmth spread up my arm, rejuvenating me. Closing my fist tightly around the medallion, I tugged sharply to break the chain and removed my hand from my shirt.

Without having to haul on Mary, I could bring my entire weight to bear against Mr Flynn. With a surge of strength that took me almost as much unawares as the creature, I yanked my left arm towards me. Mr Flynn shot through the water like a mutant torpedo, an expression of almost comic surprise on its lopsided features. I thrust my right fist forward and it struck the onrushing creature firmly in the chest.

Two things happened simultaneously. The creature's chest parted at my touch and my hand passed through the icy cavity of its torso to emerge the other side, still firmly clutching the medallion. The numbing grip on my left wrist was released and warmth surged through the arm, lending me fresh vigour.

For a moment, I stood with the creature impaled on my outstretched arm, our faces almost touching. Then it opened its mouth wide and let out a high-pitched mewl. I turned my head sharply aside to avoid the stream of putrid air that rushed from its maw in a noxious wave.

With a cry of revulsion, I placed my left hand to its shoulder and shoved, at the same time yanking back on my right arm. The creature tore free with a sticky tearing sound and toppled backwards. Water rushed through the gaping hole in its chest and it began to sink.

As I began to turn my head in search of Mary, I was distracted again by cold sharp prods to my back. I swept round to face the children who floated before me, arms outstretched in a pathetic attempt to push me. Even the baby had managed to reach me, floating on its side amidst a shoal of rags. Three pairs of red-sparking eyes regarded me with unbridled malice. Thrusting away compassion and pity for what these innocents had become, aware that I was wasting precious moments, I swept my right fist forward in an arc that sliced through the children as easily as a blue-edged scythe parts corn. Closing my mind to the carnage my fist had wrought on children, on a baby, I turned to find Mary.

She had reached the centre of the pool, but instead of despairing my heart gave a leap. The face of the late Mrs Flynn bobbed up and down in front of Mary, trying to drag her below the surface, but placid Mary had been replaced by an extremely active one. Her arms thrashed about in the water, looking as though she was resisting the creature with every fibre of her being. While I had been dispatching Mr Flynn and his children, Mary must have regained her senses.

I started to wade to her assistance but then halted in dismay. The water had reached my chin and I could venture no deeper. I could only watch and curse my inability to swim.

To my relief, it looked as though Mary would escape the creature without my aid. Leaning back in the water, she raised her legs, knees bent, and planted her feet squarely in Mrs Flynn's chest. With a grunt, Mary extended her legs, propelling herself in my direction and forcing Mrs Flynn to stumble backwards and disappear beneath the surface.

I uttered a whoop and bounced on my toes, willing Mary onwards. She turned over in the water so that she was facing me and started to pull towards me with graceful strokes. She even managed a weak grin.

She was barely four or five strokes from me when it happened. The patch of water between us hissed and bubbled and something shot upwards. My jaw dropped as I caught a glimpse of water gushing from a hole in the thing's back. A wave hit me in the face, rushing into my gaping mouth. As the late Mr Flynn landed in front of Mary, I could only cough and splutter and retch.

The creature surged forward and seized Mary by the hair in both hands. It started to swim jerkily backwards towards the centre of the pool, to where his wife was resurfacing.

Mary screamed and batted at the creature. But its grip was tight, both hands buried deep in her luxuriant mane. She scrunched her eyes in pain, unable to do anything to prevent being dragged backwards in the creature's wake.

I found my voice and yelled: "Struggle Mary! I'm coming. Struggle with all your might!"

Taking a deep breath, I plunged after her. This time I remembered to close my mouth when my head went beneath the surface. I kicked my legs and windmilled my arms, frantically trying to gain forward motion. But when I managed to raise my head clear of the water, I had barely moved. No amount of desperation was about to change the fact that I couldn't swim. What I saw filled me with fresh despair.

Mrs Flynn had moved to her husband's side and grabbed Mary by the shoulders, trying to force her beneath the surface. Mr Flynn stopped swimming and released his grip on Mary's hair with one hand, planting it on Mary's other shoulder and pressing downwards.

Mary's terrified glance found me. Her eyes brimmed with helplessness. She mouthed three words: I love you.

A moment later, she was dragged below the surface. Her gaze never left mine as she sank into the blue depths.

Unheeding the mouthfuls of water that rushed into my body, I hurled myself forwards in a series of lunging jumps. For a moment, it seemed I might make it to the spot where she had disappeared. But my momentum petered out and I felt myself sink inexorably towards the pond floor. I clutched the St Christopher tighter as though it might lend me buoyancy.

The inky depths cocooned me and my world went black.

Endings

From the familiar lushness of the grass on my face and the warmth of the sun on my back, I guessed that I was back in the Meadow. Blinking, I allowed that thought to take hold . . . then scrambled to my feet.

I looked around in all directions, desperately, but the only person I could see was Callum.

"Cal! Where's Mary? The things had her! Where is she?"

Callum shook his head. "Mary's passed on. You did all you could."

"No! . . . NO!"

Callum just looked at me and I could see the truth in the compassion of his gaze. I sank to my knees, arms coming up to cradle my head, and gave in to grief.

I don't know how much time, or whatever passes for it in the Meadow, elapsed before I became vaguely aware of my brother kneeling beside me, holding me. My mind gradually rose from the black pit it had entered and my thoughts regained some coherence.

At last I pulled away from Callum's embrace.

"Cal," I said, "I want to pass on too. I want to be with Mary."

"You can't John. Not yet. You're still alive."

"I didn't drown too?"

He shook his head. "When you awake, you will be lying on hard mud alongside a shrivelled pool of water that was once a pond. Apart from a few bruises, you'll be fine."

"Then I'll take my own life."

"Hush! Do not speak of such things. You have things to do with your life. Things to accomplish. And you will take care of Ma."

"Ma . . . I guess. . . ." I breathed out heavily. "How didn't I drown, Cal? Was it something to do with your St Christopher?"

Callum smiled, a little sadly. "Maybe. In a way. It's only a symbol, but a very powerful one."

"A symbol of what?"

Callum leaned in and placed a palm against the side of my face. "Why, little brother, a symbol of one of the most potent forces that exists. Brotherly love." He winked as he leaned back and lowered his hand. "It was certainly strong enough to foil the evil intent of those that came from Darkland." He smiled, sadly, again. "With a little help," he added.

I gasped. "*You*. You helped me. You fought Mitch. You *beat* Mitch."

"Aye. Mitch has passed on. But not, I think, to the same place I'm going."

"You're passing on too, Cal?"

"Yes. My task is completed. You are safe."

"I wish Mary was safe."

"She was not my concern. I am sorry."

"Will you see her, when you pass on?"

Callum shrugged. "I do not know."

"If you do, tell her that I love her. And that I'll be with her again . . . one day."

"I suspect she already knows. But, yes, if I see her I will tell her."

I nodded. There was more I needed to know. "Callum, why did

those things come after us? I mean, we had nothing to do with their deaths."

"Revenge. The woman had the strongest will. Three lives were to be taken in return for the lives of her three bairns. She was foiled at the last. You escaped."

"You said three lives. They only went after me and Mary."

Callum's eyes narrowed. "She hadn't told you?"

"Told me what?"

"Two souls have passed on this night. Mary and your unborn son."

I blinked. "She was pregnant?"

"It was a new soul, barely come into existence. A soul nonetheless."

My mind went momentarily blank. When the Meadow swam back into focus, Callum was speaking.

" . . . ease the pain. I must go now."

"Wait! Will . . . will I see you again, Cal?"

"Not in this place. But we will meet again, little brother. Da and Morfydd too. I am eager to go to them."

"Don't go, Callum. I need you."

"No you don't. Not any longer. You have a life to live, John. Go live it as well as I know you are capable."

He held out of his arms and I fell against him, hugging him fiercely. As we pulled apart, I had to squint against the glare. Callum was aglow. Not with the blue unwholesomeness of the Dead Lights but with a clear radiant whiteness.

He smiled, this time with happiness. I watched as the glow increased in intensity.

Callum stood in the midst of a brilliant star. He winked at me once and was gone.

Mary's body was never found. I suspect that it lay in mud at the murky bottom of the pond, weighted down by a large stone that had been employed in a similar role thirty years previously. I never felt the need to look. And I was never asked so I never told.

It was Frank Fletcher who reported her disappearance to the town's authorities. Two members of the constabulary came to investigate. I heard that neighbours of the Fletchers volunteered information that Frank Fletcher had long been known to beat his daughter and had been heard to engage in a loud and violent argument with Mary on the evening she was last seen in Tregeagle.

With no other clues as to what had become of Mary Fletcher, the constables' suspicions fell upon her father. They reasoned, so it was rumoured, that Fletcher had done away with his poor sweet daughter and had called in the constabulary to divert suspicion from him. The constables were not about to allow the absence of a body to distract their attention from the truth.

Of course, I could have informed them that Frank Fletcher had no direct involvement in Mary's death, though how I could have explained what happened without consigning myself to either becoming the chief suspect or being sent to the nearest lunatic asylum I can't begin to guess. Besides, I believed Frank Fletcher to be as culpable of the death of his daughter as if he had drowned her himself. I rejoiced when he was arrested and carted off to the town gaol, loudly protesting his innocence to deaf police ears. Although I had never met the man in the flesh, I felt that I knew him from what I had seen in Callum's vision and what I had heard issue from Martin's lips in the tavern. I felt I knew him well enough to hate him.

Frank Fletcher died in his cell two days later, awaiting trial for the murder of his daughter. The official cause of death was a heart attack, but I have often wondered whether his cell was aglow with a cold blue light at the moment of his last breath. Maybe the Flynns reaped their third life after all.

At the end of August 1947, with the heatwave a fond memory after a fortnight of rain, Ma, Gwen and I left Tregeagle with no fanfare. Arthur Bailey drove us, and a few meagre belongings, to town in his cart. He bade me a fond farewell.

I settled with Ma and Gwen for a while in Wales before wanderlust came upon me.

Gwen threw herself into the affairs of the local inhabitants and by the time of her death at the ripe old age of eighty-three had become an upstanding citizen, a pillar of the community.

Ma lived out the rest of her days in more reserved fashion, but she was happy. She had come home, where her heart had long dwelt.

As for me, I have lived a full and fulfilling life, but I am grown old and weary. My last task has been completed: to commit to the page the events of that summer, and the first and only great love of my life. It is a burden I have long held in my heart and that I am glad near the end to shed.

It is time I settled down. Buy that rose-covered cottage by the sea Mary and I once dreamed of. Write poetry.

Then I will, at last, go to her.

About the Author

When not inhabiting imaginary worlds that no others can see, Sam Kates—who swears he's sane—lives in South Wales, UK, with a computer and a family. Sometimes he joins them for meals. He has, on occasion, been known to talk to them. To his consternation, they refuse to address him as "Sam."

Author's Note

I know that book reviews on sites like Amazon and Goodreads are considered to be for the benefit of other readers, and rightly so. However, many authors also derive benefit from readers' reviews of their work and I am no exception. So if you are that way inclined, I would be delighted to receive an honest review of this work. Alternatively, if you would like to give feedback but not on a public forum, please feel free to e-mail me at samkates@hotmail.co.uk.

Thank you for purchasing and reading this book.

—Sam Kates
March 2014
samkates.co.uk

Also by this author:

The Cleansing
(Earth Haven: Book One)

Pond Life
Tales of the Wondrous and the Macabre

Lightning Source UK Ltd.
Milton Keynes UK
UKOW02f1008161114

241658UK00001B/42/P